There's No Place Like Home

Moving into my father's house hadn't been easy. I had to give away my cat Cindy. Dad was the one who broke the news. "Linda's allergic to cats. Her eyes get puffed up and she can't breathe. She's afraid to have a cat around the baby."

When a family with three kids and a golden retriever arrived to take Cindy away, I freaked out. I handed Cindy over to the girl, who was about my age. And then she was gone.

I didn't run into the house. It wasn't mine. I sat in the back yard and thought of my mother's closet, of how the sun might be streaming in right at this moment, making the carpet warm as it melted the frost on the window. My place, where I used to go when I was upset, wasn't here. Up there, in my father's house, was somebody else's room converted for me. It had been Linda's old sewing room. I replaced a sewing machine.

I wanted to be old enough right then and there to be somewhere else.

**Other Point paperbacks
you will enjoy:**

Maybe it Will Rain Tomorrow

Maybe it Will Rain Tomorrow

Jane Breskin Zalben

SCHOLASTIC INC.
New York Toronto London Auckland Sydney Tokyo

ISBN 0-590-32826-3

12 11 10 9 8 7 6 5 4 3 2 1   4   5 6 7 8 9/8 0/9

For my mother and father

Maybe it Will Rain Tomorrow

Going home was something I knew I would have to do, but I needed Aunt Ellen. She was picking me up at Dad's. I sat on the front porch quietly watching for her car. Sweat dripped between my breasts down onto my stomach, soaking my woolen sweater. My elbows dug into my thighs. Ice-cold fingers propped up my chin. I stared at the empty street of sleeping houses, all looking exactly the same: slate paths, three steps leading to stoops, two wooden columns, aluminum siding, vinyl shutters. The only thing that made one house look different from another was the color, or a flowerpot, or a jockey holding a lantern. I hated this neighborhood, and my new life.

My aunt had collected most of my things for me. Dad said that he would take care of Mom's belongings and the furniture, but first I wanted to go home without him. The thought of going there now, two months later, seeing my mother's room, and my room, frightened me.

We huddled in Aunt Ellen's VW Beetle, sipping hot chocolate from her thermos, cracking stupid jokes, as she drove along the frosted highway.

"Why do you need five people to change a lightbulb in California?"

"Why?" I asked.

"One to change the bulb and four to share the experience."

"Oh, no. Okay, I have one. This couple in their nineties go to a judge for a divorce. He asks why, and they say they wanted to wait for the children to die."

"That's awful!" screamed Aunt Ellen as she leaned on the steering wheel at the stoplight.

Turning the familiar corner, I tensed as we approached the house. Ellen's jaw tightened. The entrance to the driveway was clear. Who had shoveled the snow? Dad must have lined up one of the neighborhood kids in our absence. We walked up the front steps arm in arm. She put the key in the door and I turned to her. "I haven't been home since . . ."

"I know," she cut in. "It was difficult for me the first time, too, but once I was in your mother's room, I was calmer. My expectations were worse than the reality."

I entered the house first, wiping my feet on the mat. Then I took off my boots and put them in the front closet, as usual. It would always be my house. Mine and Mom's. A real-estate broker's card was conspicuous on the side table. I winced. Studying the steps as if they were a mountain to climb, I turned to Aunt Ellen. "I'll stay down here a minute." She understood.

"See you upstairs."

I looked around at our belongings: the funky lamp with the floral shade, a Chinese print framed in red, a brass poker still covered with ashes resting in the fireplace, Grandma's old upright piano, my Chopin book opened to a prelude I had been working on, and my metronome on the mantelpiece. I walked through the living room into Mom's favorite place, the sun porch, and sat down in her wicker chair, pushing the Moroccan pillows aside. Some of my composition pads filled with music fell from behind the pillows. When was the last time I had thought seriously about my music? Brown fern leaves from the dead hanging plants were scattered on the floor. I carefully stuffed them in a used tissue to throw away later. The cacti seemed to be managing. They didn't need much to survive. Why hadn't Dad gotten the place cleaned up? He wanted to sell it, didn't he? Maybe he was really affected by what had happened? And he wanted to leave everything untouched, as if Mom were still alive? Or was he just too busy with his own life? Her pale lipstick pressed on a cigarette butt smashed in the ashtray reminded me of her as I ran my fingers over its cloisonné pattern. Mom was a bunch of contradictions. Soy burgers and nicotine never meshed to me.

Upstairs, Aunt Ellen sat on the floor cross-legged and said, "What do you do with a dead person's clothes? They hang in the closet waiting to be worn. It's as if the person never died."

"I've been dreading this, but it's easier being here with you." I stared at my mother's bed and started to tremble.

"I feel the same way, honey."

"It's crazy the way one minute a person exists on this earth, then suddenly they don't, as if they were never here. It all seems so stupid! What's it all for?"

"I don't know," said Aunt Ellen.

I felt we were invading Mom's privacy, and in some ways we were, but it had to be done. I went to the closet door, placing my wet palm on the doorknob, and quickly jerked it open, as if I were tearing off a Band-Aid. Entering my mother's closet was like escaping to somewhere quiet and peaceful. It had racks on both sides for her clothes, lots of shelves for shoes, hats, and handbags tucked away in tissue paper. There was soft carpeting and a small window in the back. I used to feel it was one of the best places in the whole world. I'd go in there to read, or play dress-up, or be alone.

"I hid behind her skirts right here, when I was a kid," I pointed, "and wouldn't budge an inch. When she opened the door, I'd scream and slide the hangers along the pole. It was terrific. She'd yell, 'Help! They're coming to get me!' And she'd pretend to faint. I'd jump out and shout, 'It's only me!' "

Aunt Ellen paused, then continued to sort through the boxes. Then she began to cry, picking up Mom's red leather-and-wood sandals from the closet floor. The imprint of sweaty, sandy toes, from summers at Jones Beach and East Hampton, remained. "Do I save them or give them to the Salvation Army?"

"Don't you want them?" I asked, even though I half expected Mom to walk in, put them on, and say, "What are you guys doing in here?"

"No, you take them. You're the same size as your mother was, aren't you?" I didn't answer. Thank God, my aunt wasn't one of those piggy types, like some of the people who vultured through Grandma's possessions after she died, choosing them like items at a rummage sale. Aunt Ellen forced a smile and pushed my long, brown hair back from my shoulders. I decided to keep the sandals, along with the offbeat blouses that Mom found during her weekly flea-market and thrift-shop binges. Still fastened to one of the blouses was her tooled-silver-and-amethyst pin. I wrapped it in some cotton, placing it in a tiny box from Tender Buttons that I found in her dresser drawer. We neatly put my mother's life into cartons from Waldbaum's.

I wondered about what a person accumulates. Does that show the kind of person they are? Or want to be? Doug Greely, one of my parents' old friends, a banker, invested in Tiffany lamps. Forty lamps. How many did he need? He had papers for each one, like a pedigreed poodle. We knew he'd never sell one of those lamps, even though he talked about how much he could get for them. Whenever we came to visit, he liked to turn each lamp on and we'd sit in his study surrounded by colored patterns of light. And I'm sure he did that when he was alone, too. Once he came home late from work and found that robbers had vandalized his beautiful lamps. I remember that I cried. He had a heart attack, and as he recuperated, he learned to work with stained glass, repairing his lamps almost back to the way they were. I could never tell the difference. Cousin Millie saved fabric patches over the years for a quilt she never made. And then there was my mother.

I was discovering bits and pieces of her dreams as I sifted through her drawers and closet: the gourmet catering business she was going to start with our neighbor Shelly. The two of them had more fun talking about it than actually doing it. They pored through cookbooks, explored quaint little restaurants, tested out their recipes on me. I held a sample menu of stiff parchment in my hands. Mom had lettered it in delicate calligraphy. *Crème aux bananes.* Why do bananas and cream sound so much fancier in French? And *les fraises* taste better served in champagne glasses than out of the strawberry box, or maybe even right off the plant runners? Because Mom said they did? They never got the business going.

A yellowed clipping from the local newspaper showed a photo of my mother smiling. The caption below the photo read: "Marion Corey planting the first daffodil bulb at our recently restored pond." I remember when Mom joined the fight for cleaning up that mud pile that had become a landfill of beer cans and gum wrappers. I grinned at the headline. *"Duck Pond Dredged. Ducks Dive Deliriously."*

I fumbled with a pot holder Mom used in demonstrations for her volunteer work in the arts-and-crafts program at the Senior Citizens Center. "How many crocheted clowns and knitted afghans can one person make?" I asked. Bored, she left after a week. I sat and thought. There was the part-time job at the combination antique store / picture frame / ice-cream-soda place, but she hated selling, and quit. I found the catalogue for the Adult Education courses at my high school. Mom signed up for a Great Books Discussion Group. She said that the leader smoked a pipe, and as he leaned back in his seat in a pensive posture, his eyes became small and beady. We laughed as she imitated what she called the two categories in this all-women group: the intellectual tea drinkers, and the frosted-hair coffee-cuppers. Mom felt these efforts of hers were all a step up from the ultimate fate of a divorced woman in her circumstances: self-help or consciousness-raising groups, Wednesday-lunch bridge games, bowling leagues, aerobic dancing, exercise classes, or Friday-night bar hopping. Dad once called Mom a professional beginner.

Finally, she seemed to have discovered where she belonged: a post-graduate course in printmaking in Manhattan. I stared at the lithographs in the folder in front of me. And the etching of my father from a sketch she had done years earlier. She was happy during those months and came home very excited from each class. Tired of going into the city twice a week from where we lived in Westchester, she didn't register for the second term. Instead, she worked in a small gallery in town, hanging other people's art.

I pulled out unfinished canvases that were stacked against the wall behind long dresses and bathrobes. I wrapped her Bachelor of Fine Arts diploma from Sarah Lawrence in newspaper so the glass wouldn't break. A diploma in a simple black frame. Tucked away.

Tossing aside the Adult Ed catalogue and crummy pot holder, I thought, "How would Mom have liked to be put in the position of deciding whether or not to throw out my tennis sneakers with the holes near the big toes?" Choosing and judging what should end up in the garbage and what should be spared? I wanted to keep all the memories.

"Look at this!"

Aunt Ellen leaned over my shoulder as I read:

> *Roses are red*
> *Violets are blue*
> *In years from now*
> *I'll still love you.*

> A Zillion Hugs and Kisses,
> Beth   xxxxxxxxxxxxxx

"It's a valentine I made for her when I was small." I was surprised that she had kept it. A red crayoned heart with tiny arrows embroidered in hot-pink yarn. "Corny, huh?"

"I think it's kind of sweet," said Ellen.

"My thesis for kindergarten." Would I receive one of these someday? It was special, and I wasn't going to throw it away.

I also found my first piano-recital program. Beth Corey. Number Seven. *Für Elise* by Beethoven. My fluffy dress had stuck to the back of my thighs from sweat, staying there as I got up to take a bow. Every year, for as long as I can remember, the first Sunday in May, Mom, Dad, and I sat waiting in some school auditorium for my turn to play. We'd go out for ice-cream sodas afterwards. Our Sundays stopped when I was ten and there was no longer the three of us. Mom and Dad had separated.

I glimpsed up, remembering where I was, and it was now. Beth Corey. Sixteen. Hanging from a nail near a back shelf, a blue satin sachet was tied with a pale pink ribbon.

"You know, Mom's closet never reeked of mothballs like those blue-haired ladies in violet sweaters. It reminds me of a gerbil cage."

"Cedar does that," said Aunt Ellen. "My sister was jasmine through and through. Don't you smell perfume on her things?" She put a scarf to her nose.

"Yes. And her smelly armpits." We both laughed. "Mom didn't believe in deodorants. Chemicals. She'd say, '*Au naturel*. We're animals anyway. It turns men on! Forget this advertising garbage! *Eau de cochon!*' And she'd wink in a wicked little way."

Suddenly Aunt Ellen stopped folding and sorting. "Marion and I were sisters. Why didn't she call? Let me know if things were so awful?"

"She didn't tell me, Aunt El, and I lived with her. Maybe she didn't want to upset you?"

"Upset me," she repeated. "I, of all people, should have known something was up."

"Do you therapists have crystal balls? Mom kept things inside. Sometimes people hurt so much they don't want to dump all those bad feelings onto the next person. I know. I'm there right now."

Aunt Ellen put down what she was doing and hugged me. "That's enough for now. Let's go downstairs and have a cup of tea."

"Do we have hot water and all?" I asked as we walked down the steps.

"I imagine so. Everything seems to be working. Your father left the heat on so the pipes wouldn't freeze. Did you know he just put the house on the market? We should take what we want today before some cleaning service sterilizes the place."

"I noticed an agent's card on the way in. I wish I could live here forever."

"No, you don't. Even if your mother was alive."

"Rose hip or Lipton?" I asked, poking in the tins lined up above the kitchen sink.

"Give me the hard stuff. I need the caffeine. I feel completely drained."

"So do I." I filled the teapot with water and then sat down across from Aunt Ellen. The late-afternoon light shined on her and she looked so much like Mom. Tilting my head sideways on my fist, I rested my elbow on the round butcher-block table. From one of the cartons I had carried downstairs, I took out an old picture postcard from a vacation my mother had taken alone in Florida after the divorce. Mom was a sucker for palm trees. That and piña coladas. They went to her head. Dad said that she wasn't responsible for what she did when she hit balmy air. Once, when I was seven, we danced wildly on sand dunes in the early morning, and made angels on the beach with our bodies. On that same vacation, we swam in the motel pool late at night while Dad slept in our room. And then we went to a nearby drive-in movie, where we ate fried clams, tacos, and pizza, gorging ourselves in the front seat of a rented car, sipping thick vanilla milk shakes. Mom would take me out for breakfast, and I saved those little packaged jellies they serve you with eggs as if they were precious jewels glistening in their containers. She seemed so easily satisfied, but I guess she wasn't. I stared at Mother's kitchen for the very last time, with the teas and spices in neat rows tucked in Ball jars and ceramic crocks.

Snowflakes dusted the windshield. Aunt Ellen drove me back to Dad's. Carly Simon was singing *Haven't Got Time for the Pain* on the radio. The backseat of the car was filled with packed cartons tied with cord. Some of them were marked "Beth." The rest were marked "Marion." Aunt Ellen saw me staring at them. For now, they would remain closed.

"I'll look through the boxes again in a few weeks, when I have the strength. Don't worry. I'll take good care of them. They're important to both of us. Call you tomorrow to see how you are. Take it easy." She waved goodbye and threw me a kiss. I choked as I saw the burgundy car turn the corner. She was heading back to her one-bedroom apartment in Manhattan, where she lived alone. There wasn't enough room for me there, but I fantasized about living with her.

two

Sleeping in Dad's house was difficult. I was glad I had taken my pillow with me. What you remember is dumb sometimes. Mom had splurged on two soft goose-down pillows during a January white sale at Bloomingdale's just a few weeks before she died. A faint rosebud pattern on the case resembled my baby blanket. Linda gave me one of those crummy blue-and-white-striped foam jobs, the kind manufactured for the motel industry. Her pillow conjured up nights at sleep-away camp, out on the rocky ground. I returned it to the top of the linen closet, on the back shelf, hoping it would go unnoticed.

The light from the street lamp shone through the window. Leaf patterns danced across the ceiling and walls. I lay in bed under my old patchwork quilt. A branch thumped against the shingles and shutters, reminding me of all the unfamiliar night-times spent in this house, in this bedroom.

I missed the beige, faded wallpaper in my old room. Mom had saved an extra roll or two. I'd ask Dad, and of course Linda, if I could put it up, fig-uring since I was here I'd better try and make my-self comfortable. I had my rocker from home, but there I had had an open view of the sky past Mrs. Wheaton's yard. Here I faced the house next door and somebody else's window. I had all my posses-sions: rocks, shells from summer vacations at Cape Cod; miniature enameled and lacquered boxes; apothecary and essence bottles in red, blue, purple, amber, and clear; cheap vases; tons of chewed-up paperbacks; old books from when I was a kid; yel-lowed sheet music; records and tapes. They hadn't found their niches; I left them in cartons.

As I drifted off to sleep, the boiler stirred. A monster patiently waiting in the basement. It seemed to shake the whole house. The floorboards creaked below my bed and sounded like popcorn frying.

That refrigerator drove me nuts! Our fridge was old reliable. White. Not color-coordinated. I didn't hear ice cubes dropping or water trickling. I couldn't believe I heard theirs all the way up here. Sure, it was a drag to defrost ours. Mom used to blow her hair dryer on the icebergs that built up on the trays. "We'll get electrocuted someday!" I warned. So we converted to pots of hot water. We'd run back and forth from the refrigerator to the kitchen sink. Dad knew when Mom decided to defrost the freezer. "Did the Titanic sink again?" he'd ask, tiptoeing over the puddles and soggy dish towels. "Mom's a closet penguin," I said. Mom and I would get it mopped up before dinner.

God, how I wanted to be home again, for all this to be a dream, a nightmare. And I'd hear Mom screaming upstairs, "Hey, cutie, get your ass on out of bed, or you'll be late for school."

The next morning, I woke up to buzzing lawn mowers. Gardening day in suburbia. Cleaning up from the long winter. The alarm clock read eight. I rolled over, hoping I would fall back to sleep. Dad lived on the most perfect block in the world. Neat little cemetery plots. Blacktop driveways, electronic garage doors, underground sprinkler systems, and wall-to-wall sod.

It was the first Saturday morning in April, when you get a taste of what's to come. I leaned toward the windowsill to see the thermometer. 73 degrees. I grabbed my T-shirt from the nearby bureau, pushing the curtains back slightly as I rubbed the sand out of the corners of my eyes. That's when I saw him for the first time. My best friend, Nance, from home, would have said, "What a hunk!" He was mowing the lawn across the street. Thank God for neat little cemetery plots. I couldn't take my eyes off him.

This was definitely a no-jacket day. "Don't go out like that!" Mom would shout. "You'll be sick by Sunday." Sure enough, Monday morning I'd wake up with a sore throat and an ache in my glands just below my ears. I'd be in bed until Tuesday with a heating pad wrapped around my neck and Kleenex stuffed up my nostrils. She would bring in boiled salt water every hour and a pinch of aspirin for me to gargle with. I knew I should listen to the voice of my mother in me and wear a sweater, but the T-shirt showed off my breasts.

My body raced. I could almost feel my blood flowing as I ran around. The only other time I had a feeling this wonderful was when I played a solo at a school assembly and everyone stood up and applauded.

I opened the window to get a better view. This hunk had his work shirt unbuttoned, with the sleeves rolled up. He had the kind of arms I liked. Strong and hairy. Not apey, not bald. Just the right amount. I wondered if he had nice hands. A real nut, I thought. He's crazier than me. It isn't that warm. His stomach was flat and muscular. I could see the ripples of his ribs as he mowed the lawn. The Beach Boys filled the air from his portable radio. God, was he good-looking! Where were my jeans? I hoped they weren't in the dirty laundry. They were on the other side of the bed, under the dust ruffle. And my sneakers? Maybe they're too klutzy? Clogs? I'd wear Mom's sandals. I have nice toes.

I ripped off the T-shirt and put on my mauve leotard. It made me feel artistic. Turning sideways, I looked at the profile of my body in the mirror. That was more like it. Much sexier. Then I took a hand mirror to see the back of my hair. As I brushed it, I glanced down at my behind. It looked sort of nice in jeans, but I wished it would shrink along with my jeans in the dryer. Why couldn't it be smaller?

Nearly piercing them a second time, I slipped gold hoop earrings through my ears. It reminded me of the fights with Mom about getting them pierced when I was eleven. Everyone was having them done at Hamler's Jewelry Emporium. It was free if you bought a pair of earrings over $9.99. Nance's pure 14-karat-gold ones turned to silver and her earlobes became puffy and green near the little holes. I never told Mom, but I argued for the same opportunity. She finally gave in on one condition: Dr. Toh would do it in her office under sterile conditions. She bought me gold-and-jade posts for my twelfth birthday that year. I rushed once again to the window. The sun was still shining, but it was beginning to drizzle. The truck, the tools, the gardening paraphernalia had all disappeared. I couldn't believe the fuss I went to. What a jerk I was. To think, two minutes before you could have peeled me off the ceiling. I spent the rest of the day in my room trying to write some music, but the most I ended up with was one page. The wastebasket was full to the brim.

three

Moving into my father's house hadn't been easy. It wasn't home. I had to give away my cat Cindy. Dad was the one who broke the news. "Linda's allergic to cats. Her eyes get puffed up and she can't breathe. She's afraid to have a cat around the baby."

I lost my mother and my pet. And I loved Cindy so. She'd curl up next to me on the bed, roll on her back, and snore. Her body became warm and heavy as she stretched out, crowding me. Mom used to call her the Hog. I complained to Aunt Ellen on the telephone. "Who will comb her fur like I did? Give her baths in the kitchen sink with Johnson's Baby Shampoo? Wrap her in a terry-cloth robe afterwards, so she won't catch a cold? Who will treat an animal like that?"

"Someone crazy." She chuckled. "You sound like a mother."

I begged Linda. "Please, I'll vacuum every day and bathe Cindy once a week. I promise to dust everything and clip her claws so she won't shred the carpeting or scratch the dining-room chairs." I was tempted to say, I'll pick up the dander with tweezers, but I didn't.

"I'm sorry, I've tried, but I know if a cat's in a house, even when I visit someone. I can sense it. They're so sneaky, hiding out under some bed or couch waiting to pounce." Linda had a sixth sense. Cat sense. "No matter how clean a house is," she went on, "I have to leave."

Soon after I came to live with them, the ad went into the Sunday *Times* under the pet-adoption column: CHILD HEARTBROKEN. ADORABLE CAT SEEKS LOVING HOME. GOOD WITH CHILDREN. The night before she left me, I packed her brown wicker bed, yellow plastic bowl, and plaid woolen blanket, the one she'd had since she was born. When a family with three kids and a golden retriever arrived, I freaked out. Cindy would never be able to tolerate a dog. I thought, I should be grateful. Someone is taking in my full-grown cat. But I wasn't. They didn't raise her from a little kitten. It was as if they were stealing her. I envisioned her starving, scrounging for scraps in garbage cans. They will take her up to their farm in the country and make her a mouser. A barn cat.

I handed Cindy over to the girl, who was about my age. Cindy's black-and-white face with its pink nose peeked out of the plastic carrying case. They put her in the back of the Jeep. I hoped she wasn't panting as she does when she gets frightened. And then she was gone. Why did I even look? I didn't run into the house. It wasn't mine. I sat in the back yard and thought of my mother's closet, of how the sun might be streaming in right at this moment, making the carpet warm as it melted the frost on the window. My place, where I used to go when I was upset, wasn't here. Up there, in my father's house, was somebody else's room converted for me. It had been Linda's old sewing room. I replaced a sewing machine.

Spool by spool, she had taken the thread down off her pegboard and placed each spool neatly in an old cookie tin. "Can I put my Grateful Dead poster up on the pegboard?" I asked reluctantly, as she jabbed pins into the cushion.

Linda turned sharply. "Why not, I won't be needing it any more." It was the "any more" that got to me. I knew I was being touchy, but I wanted to smash her in the face. I couldn't help it. I wanted to say, "I don't want to use your cruddy pegboard, I don't want to be here." Instead, I watched her make room in her dresser full of fabrics and stray buttons for my sweaters and pajamas, and in her closet, now emptied of the sewing dummy and Vogue patterns, for my clothes and shoes. Her clothes were in vinyl garment bags, skirts separated from pants and shirts. Categorized. Mom kept her clothes loose and free.

In the corner, toward the back of the bottom drawer, I discovered some forgotten tiny mother-of-

22

pearl buttons. I ran after Linda, handing her the card that displayed them in two neat rows. She thanked me and sighed, looking down at them and then toward my room, and said they'd be perfect for a sweater she was crocheting for Lisa. Dad hauled the sewing machine downstairs to his study, which was already tight, moving his own desk to the darker side.

"It's better this way. I can sew late at night, downstairs, without disturbing anyone."

Then why hadn't she done it before? I wanted to be old enough right then and there to be somewhere else.

We never really hit it off. When I first met Linda, I was twelve. It was summertime. I felt good because Mom didn't send me to camp that year. I could sleep late and I didn't have to take swimming tests and eat peanut-butter sandwiches. Dad and I planned to meet at the Central Park Zoo. There was this tall, thin, blond lady with him. They were getting married, buying a house on Long Island, and planning to have a family. I didn't see Dad that often during the two years after he left Mom, before Linda, but I still felt suddenly deserted that day, as if I had only one parent. I knew I wasn't going to like Linda when she had made a big fuss about my father and me eating hot dogs from a street vendor. With Mom, it would have been the impending danger of nitrites. But with Linda it was, where had those frankfurters been and who had touched them? What microorganisms were floating in their steamy baths and spreading on those stale buns? When you got down to it, I really disliked Linda because she looked perfect, as if she had walked out of a Breck commercial. How did she get her hair so bright and yellow and shiny? I was hot and sticky at the end of that day in the park. Linda looked fresh. Perky. I went home, took a bath, and told my mother what a mistake Dad was making.

My father gave up his studio sublet in the city, near his office, and that marked the end of our rare meetings alone on a vacation or weekend. I stopped worrying about the silences between our sentences because Linda was always there to fill them. I never dreamed, during the four years I was making excuses as to why I couldn't visit for a holiday, that I'd be having this conversation with Linda about what I could put on a wall in my own bedroom.

One night, at dinner, I thought hard about living with them.

Dad asked Linda, "How was your day?"

Linda's eyes darted toward me. I shifted mine down to my lamb chops lined up on my plate.

"Oh, the usual. I'm knocked out. Lisa's crawling into everything. I had to fight her for the Drano."

"I'm sorry, sweetheart. I know it's hard right now. She'll grow up faster than you want her to. Look at Beth. I can't believe I have a sixteen-year-old daughter. Children really mark your age. Did you get a chance to take my pants to the cleaners? And buy the spark plugs for the lawn mower?"

"No," said Linda, tightening her lips.

"It's all right. I can take care of it on the weekend. How was your day, Beth? You're going to begin a new school soon. That should be exciting."

"I guess so."

"What subjects are you taking?"

"I don't know yet."

And the conversation ended there.

I couldn't believe that every night he discussed his dull law cases with Linda. *Schmuck* vs. *Yahoo*. And she listened. "The merger's going through," I overheard him say as they were stacking the dishes into the dishwasher.

"Does that mean a Christmas bonus?"

"Could be. They might give us a trip to Guadeloupe. Everything included down to a rum-swizzle party."

"Boy, could I use that. Just the two of us, again."

What was I doing here? With these people? The "two" of them? I remembered their small wedding. How Dad's parents, Grandma and Grandpa Corey, picked me up on their way from the airport in a taxi. And Mom wasn't there. She went to a movie that day. Dad had invited her. For me.

"I'll have only a few meetings. And there will be other wives, too. Tom's wife is an interesting girl."

Hasn't she reached puberty? Interesting *woman.* That's if she is, I thought. I reached into the refrigerator for an apple, and an orange rolled onto the floor.

"What do you want?" Linda asked.

"An apple."

"I left them on the dining-room table."

"I like them cold."

"Then put some in the fruit-and-vegetable bin. Don't hold the refrigerator door open, the cool air is escaping."

Linda bugged me. My mother didn't care about that one corporate vacation a year. She wanted to change our lives from day to day. It was a never-ending battle. Mom always wanted Dad to work for a place like Legal Aid, representing juveniles or civil-rights cases. Dad chose corporate law when he was in college and they were going together. He wanted stability instead of a practice for the good of society.

My father had the right to do what he wanted with his life, but down deep I agreed with my mother. She didn't think he ever felt happy. I don't know. Seeing him with Linda now, I felt he lost his chance to be someone better than he was.

Later that evening, I watched Dad and Linda with Lisa. My father stacked colorful alphabet blocks on the living-room floor. Lisa grabbed one, put it on top of another block, as Linda clapped and hugged her with such excitement. Lisa clapped, imitating her. Linda smoothed back the fuzzy crop of hair that made Lisa look like a newborn duckling and kissed her on the forehead, the way my mother had done to me so often. I ached for that closeness, and it hurt knowing I'd never have it again with my mother. Maybe Mom felt she could leave me now, now that I was old enough to take care of myself physically. Why didn't she understand my other needs? If only she knew I wasn't ready to be separated from her. She had to have known that. She was my mother.

I sat in my room, away from Dad, Linda, and Lisa, and thought about what had happened. "To commit suicide. What a crazy expression," I said aloud. "To commit," according to Webster's dictionary, "is to intrust . . . signifies to put into the care of another, implying a degree of confidence in the person to whom the trust is given." I laughed bitterly.

four

April 5 was my first day at Bleeker High School. Almost three months left until the end of the term. I hadn't been able to face a classroom for the past two months. Dad got a doctor's note and worked it out so I could have time to recuperate. I could always make up the assignments in summer school if I had to.

Lisa was bawling in the nursery, next to my room. Linda shuffled down the hall to get the bottle she had sterilized the night before. Once, when I first came to live with them, I walked in on Linda breast-feeding Lisa in the living room. She asked, "Could you hold Lisa while I change breasts? It would make it easier." I didn't know what she meant, but I uncomfortably bent down, picked up Lisa's fragile body, and held her like a china cup. Linda unfastened her nursing bra, which was some contraption, and took Lisa from my unsteady arms, placing her at the other breast. I stared at the fireplace behind her, not knowing where to look. She covered herself with a shawl and continued to nurse. Usually, she wore shirts that unbuttoned in the front, so you couldn't see anything. I was relieved. I wondered if I was breast-fed. I never thought of asking my mother. Lisa fell asleep. Linda closed her eyes, leaned her head against the back of the wing chair, and smiled.

Today the house was hopping at Lisa's 6 a.m. feeding. Dad was already in the shower. Linda was clanging pots downstairs. I couldn't believe it. As long as I lived here, I was destined to wake up early. Lawn mowers buzzing. Babies yapping. Lisa's cries got louder. I heard a scream from the kitchen. "Oh damn! Be-e-th! Could you look in on Lisa? I broke her bottle and have to make another one."

"All right," I shouted back. Didn't she know we're living in the age of plastic? I crawled out of bed, put on my cranberry velour bathrobe, lifting up the hood. The morning chill disappeared. All warm and cuddly, I felt like a baby snuggled in a blanket. When I went into Lisa's room, I was sick. The diaper pail was enough to knock me out. I decided to let Linda do the honors.

Linda looked tired as she changed Lisa's diaper, and the day had hardly begun. "What a cute little chicken mobile above Lisa's crib," I lied. It played "Old MacDonald Had a Farm" when you wound it up. In the center of four fluffy innocent chicks was a rooster.

"It's precious, isn't it?" Linda smiled, cooing as she cradled the baby in her arms. Lisa rooted with her lips and made sucking noises as she aimed for the nipple. "Aren't you happy as a clam now, you little peanut? If only everything in life could be this simple," she sighed.

I walked out of the room, and then turned around. Linda sat on a window seat singing a lullaby as she rocked Lisa. It was like a medieval fresco, the morning light glowing on both of them, as if they were the only two people in the universe. Mother and child.

"Am I jealous?" I murmured to myself, returning to my room. I closed the door, then stubbed my toe on the edge of the bed and stood bent over rubbing it. As I sat down in my rocker, my little toe stopped throbbing. "Well, it's that time, folks, I better get it together for school."

"I'll drive you along the same route the bus goes," said Dad.

"I'm not a child. If you tell me where the stop is, I can take the bus myself."

"I'll *show* you where to get the bus, it's a public one, and I'll drive you to school today, so you know where you're going. Stop being so independent. You'll have time enough for that tomorrow."

I stared out the window and shut up because I did feel nervous about getting lost the first day. The high school was close, but I didn't want to take a chance on being late. Once I got used to it, I figured I'd ride my bike. Back home it was hilly. Here it was flat and boring. It would be a piece of cake. A ladybug flew in, landing on my overalls. I counted the spots. Seven. My lucky number. Was this an omen? I looked up out of the open window at all the kids. It was a sea of denim. "That was fast."

"I told you it was nearby. Just a little tricky since all the streets look the same out here. Do you want me to come in with you?" asked Dad as he pulled up to the curb.

"No, you'll miss your train."

"Somehow the world will go on."

I couldn't believe this was coming from him.

"I'll be fine. I really will."

I looked him in the eye, so he'd know I meant it; I wasn't sure I did. He patted me on the back as I got out of the car.

"Good luck," he yelled, leaning out of the window.

He waited until I got to the door.

I waved goodbye. I was on my own.

five

I sized up Bleeker. My old school, Hyland North, was made of grayish-blue stone. Carved gargoyles ominously guarded the large wooden entrance doors. Heavy Gothic black wrought-iron hardware gave the place a sense of stability. Ivy crawled up the sides. Mom said that it was "veddy" Westchester. The many steps up to the front made me think of a castle in Ireland or a cloister in France. I used to pretend I was an heiress in a lavish mansion built into a cliff overlooking the ocean. My stomach growled, interrupting my 8 a.m. daydream.

Bleeker had no steps. You went straight in. It was glass and brick, with newly planted rhododendrons and spindly fir trees. Inside was a jumble of exposed pipes painted in slick primary colors. It was kind of exciting, like being in a discotheque, or fast-food joint. Mom would have called it "McDonald's modern." Large block letters and arrows directed the traffic flow. I thought it would be a cinch getting around, but I was overwhelmed by the crowd after being out of school for two months and returning to a new one. It was as if I was outside of myself watching some other person going through the motions. It was really weird.

"Excuse me," I said. "Could you . . ." The girl passed by. "Hello." I tapped someone lightly on the shoulder. So gently, he didn't feel it. A teacher came up to me. "You look confused. Can I help you in any way?" She resembled Aunt Ellen, the way she smiled softly.

"Oh, yes. Where's the principal's office?" Just making contact made me feel a little more secure.

"Right there." She pointed directly in front of me and I went in.

"I'm Beth Corey. I'm a new student here," I said to a secretary behind an electric typewriter. She immediately clicked it off as I spoke to her. Her hair was in a French knot. She wore glasses that were salmon-colored on the top of the frame and clear on the bottom. Little rhinestones on the wings of the frames sparkled in the fluorescent light. A string held them around her neck. A tissue was balled up and tucked in the sleeve of her white angora sweater. She looked like she had stepped out of my seventh-grade hygiene book.

"Is there a parent, adult, or legal guardian accompaning you?" she asked in a nasal lisp. I hadn't been asked that since I was about twelve.

"What is this? A movie with a PG rating?" I muttered.

"What did you say?"

"I said, I'm alone."

She raised one eyebrow. "I'll get the guidance counselor."

"Not the principal?"

But she had already disappeared into a maze of glass partitions. A tall, thin, thirtyish woman came over. "You must be Beth Corey."

I looked up from the floor.

"I'm Ms. Rose, your guidance counselor. I have your records from Hyland North. Come into my office, dear, we'll talk."

I hated when anyone called me dear. I followed Ms. Rose into her plant-filled haven.

"It seems that you have an extremely good aptitude for music," she went on. I listened to her impatiently. I wasn't in the mood. The phone rang. Ms. Rose turned away and talked quietly into the receiver. I could feel knots in my stomach. "I have to go, Cynthia, I'll see you at lunch. A student's in my office." She faced me. "And I imagine you'll want to take your electives in that area?"

"What area?" I asked.

"Music. It says here that you play a few instruments."

"Mmm."

"What kinds?"

"Piano, guitar, and flute, a little."

"How varied. What a talented young lady."

"Ms. Rose, do you have my program for the rest of the semester?"

"It's right here. We can arrange your music classes during your free periods. These are the required courses." She handed me the computer printout. I glanced at my schedule. "I don't take Spanish."

"I'll see what I can do, there wasn't any room in the French classes."

"I've no desire to learn Spanish."

"You should. Especially since we live only a half hour from New York City." What did that have to do with anything? Montmartre was what I wanted, not Mount Morris Park.

"You've missed homeroom, so I'll bring you to your first class at the end of the hall. I've blocked in music theory." At least it wasn't trigonometry.

"You won't be bored. Mr. Wheldon is an experienced, professional musician. He performed at Lincoln Center once. We're lucky to have him on our faculty." So why's he teaching high school, my mother would have asked? As if in answer, Ms. Rose continued, "Every summer, Dave Wheldon goes to Tanglewood and gives concerts. He's been playing in a quartet for years and lives for those summers in-between teaching." Ms. Rose babbled on as we walked. Suddenly she stopped and gestured with a sweeping of her arm, as if I should enter on stage. "Here it is!"

Ms. Rose opened the door. Everyone turned. Mr. Wheldon hesitated as he pointed to a C-sharp-major chord on the blackboard. A boy was standing. From the back he looked familiar. His blond hair hung over the collar of his Western shirt and swept around as he turned to stare at me. It looked like the boy who had been mowing the lawn across the street from Dad's just this weekend. My heart started pounding.

"Have a seat." Mr. Wheldon nodded and said casually, "I'll see you at the end of class. Jonathan, please go on."

Jonathan. His name fit. He looked like a Jonathan. He qualified for Nance's three Rs. And they weren't reading, writing, and 'rithmetic. She said that a guy was a hunk if he was rugged, raunchy, and refined, which meant he had to be sexy, intelligent, and a class act rolled into one. Jonathan had a large, strong body and a deep voice that sounded like a newscaster's. Larry, my old telephone boyfriend from home, had a voice that always cracked when he got uptight. And he didn't shave yet. So Nance said that he didn't qualify for "hunkhood."

Nance's boyfriend, Irwin, aside from having what his mother referred to as overactive sebaceous glands, what the ads called seborrhea, what I called pimples and Nance diplomatically called teenage acne, and what my mother diagnosed as an overindulgent appetite for Milky Ways, was not a hunk. He also started telling dirty jokes when he turned fifteen. He was really gross. Nance couldn't even repeat them to me over the phone for fear the operator was listening in, or the C.I.A. was tapping us. I guess Jonathan was the first true hunk I ever saw.

For the next forty minutes, until the bell rang, I didn't hear anything. I watched Jonathan. It was really him.

I'd have to call Nance when I got home from school to tell her. I hadn't made any friends on the Island yet and I was bursting to tell someone. I knew she'd faint when I told her about him.

Each day, I sat a few rows behind Jonathan, where I could stare at him. He would lean slightly forward when he became interested in what Mr. Wheldon was saying. The lines in his forehead would wrinkle around the top of his nose where his eyebrows met, making me feel he was very into what was going on at the time. What Nance called "an intense person." When Mr. Wheldon said something funny, Jonathan would sink into his seat, his long legs stretched out, his head thrown to one side, back a little, and laugh. There was something nice and warm and open about Jonathan's face. An intelligent sparkle in his eyes like that in a child's. Best of all, Jonathan had nice hands. Hands that had been exercised, that showed strength. They weren't lean, or short and stubby with bitten nails. They were beautiful when he played the flute in front of the class to demonstrate one of Mr. Wheldon's points in theory.

On Friday, at the end of my first week of school, I tried to get up the nerve to talk to Jonathan and tell him how well I thought he played, but the bell rang to change classes before I had collected my things. He had wrapped up his flute and was gone by the time I turned around.

six

Getting up in the morning was so different. I could hardly think of anything but Jonathan. I set the alarm clock to go off early Saturday morning. I was going into Manhattan to have breakfast with Aunt Ellen.

The sky was white. I couldn't tell what kind of a day it was going to be, so I stuffed a hooded sweat shirt into my shoulder bag. I rode my bike to the station. The stores in the shopping center were locked. Even the deli wasn't open yet. It was a street from *The Twilight Zone*, dead and quiet, as if there had been a plague while I slept and now I was the only one left alive.

I chained my ten-speed to the bike rack and waited for the train to pull in. The weekend schedule was posted on the door. I'd have to kill about fifteen minutes before catching the 7:39 to Penn Station. I leaned against a pole on the deserted platform and closed my eyes, enjoying the warmth of what was turning out to be a beautiful spring day. When I opened my eyes, some guy was sitting on the steps of a pedestrian overpass that crossed the track from the parking lot to the platform. A long, thin case lay next to him on the ground as he read a newspaper. A steaming Styrofoam cup was near his boot. When he picked it up to take a sip, I realized that it was Jonathan.

I didn't know where to hide. Should I run back? Catch the next train out? That was an hour later. I had to meet Aunt Ellen at around a quarter to nine. It would be too late; I couldn't reach her on the phone. Ellen was already jogging near the reservoir or somewhere on Riverside Drive. I hid behind a pole. As it got closer to 7:39, more people drifted onto the platform, helping to camouflage me.

I looked down at the tracks. The train was coming. The platform shook. Jonathan glanced up from his paper and stood up as it pulled in. He saw me and smiled. I pretended to look past him at the train, as if I didn't see him and had something important on my mind. He shrugged his shoulders. As the doors opened, I ran into the car and slumped down in the seat. Suddenly the heavy steel door in-between the cars opened. It was the conductor collecting the tickets.

Out of breath, I sighed. Right behind him was Jonathan. I stopped breathing. Coronary time. Jonathan smiled again. He was going to stop. Why couldn't he be shy, how could he do this? I wanted to be left alone to stare out the window aimlessly for the next thirty-six minutes. "Please keep going," I prayed. He leaned over, his hand rested on the back of the seat, almost touching my hair. "Aren't you in my first period music theory?"

"Yes," I said.

"I'm Jonathan Schein," he said, and smiled.

What a smile. I melted.

"I had to walk back. This is a nonsmoking car and the other one wasn't. It smelled really foul in there, like a poolroom."

"Oh, I didn't notice." I looked up and saw NO SMOKING.

"What's your name again?" he asked, and smiled for a second time.

Didn't his cheeks hurt from all that smiling? I was annoyed he didn't know my name. "Beth Corey," I said softly.

"Hmm?"

"Beth Corey," I repeated.

"Oh. Is that short for Elizabeth?"

"No, it's short for Corinne."

"You're kidding."

"Yeah," I said uncomfortably, "forget it. It was a stupid joke. No, it's always been just Beth."

"It's a nice name."

"Thanks. So is Jonathan. Do people shorten it to Jon or Jonny?"

"No. I hate that. It is Jonathan."

"Good," I said.

There was an awkward pause.

"Can I sit down here?" He pointed to a seat diagonally across from me.

"Sure." What would I say for the next half hour?

He put his stuff on the seat next to him, close to the window, away from the outside aisle.

"For protection." My eyes darted to the black case and backpack. "It's my flute and music books. I always get paranoid about someone ripping it off. As if thieves are aspiring flutists."

"My mother used to be afraid all robbers are art collectors. She painted a little."

"That's funny. My mom thinks someone's going to run off with her piano. I could just see them squeezing it through the front door."

We both laughed.

"Why are you taking your flute on the train?"

"I'm going into the city for a lesson," he answered.

"So early? Where is it?"

"Juilliard. I go there on Saturday mornings."

I got curious because he had been mowing the lawn on a Saturday morning. I didn't say anything. It wasn't any of my business, but I was dying to ask.

"You must be good," I said.

"I have a scholarship. I'm lucky, because money is really tight sometimes in our house."

"Oh, that's great. About the scholarship, I mean."

"What are you doing out so early on a Saturday? I wish I was back in bed." He yawned.

"You have a choice."

Jonathan smirked. "You're right. I guess I want to be on this train at the crack of dawn and schlep into Manhattan to play a flute at 9:00 in the morning in a rehearsal room without any windows or ventilation on a beautiful day when I could be lying on the beach in the sun."

"But you do."

"Our first fight?" His eyes twinkled.

"I guess so!" I laughed.

"Why *are you* going in?"

"To have breakfast with my aunt. I'm meeting her at some café at Seventy-sixth and Columbus. I have the name written down."

"We could walk or take the subway up together. I'm heading in that direction, too."

I nodded. "Let's walk. It's such a sunny day. I love the city when it's empty in the early morning. In the suburbs, it's like *Invasion of the Body Snatchers*. In the city, the streets belong to people walking their dogs, riding their bicycles, or jogging. It smells of coffee and breakfast, not buses, taxis, and herds of shoppers. I feel like it's mine so early."

"I know what you mean, but I like walking to the station, smelling the freshly cut grass, hearing the sailboats clang, and seeing the water on the bay."

Coming from Jonathan, it didn't sound mushy.

The train entered the tunnel. My greatest fear vanished. I talked nonstop for the entire trip and it was pretty easy after I got into it. When we got off the train and went up the deserted escalator to Seventh Avenue, Jonathan squinted into the glaring sun. "What weather. It should be a terrific day for picking up some extra cash."

"How's that?"

"I play flute in a group with three other guys and a girl I know from Juilliard. We meet on Fifth Avenue if it's sunny, winter or summer. We jam, or play pieces. Make some money from the people passing by."

"Street musicians."

"Yep. That's us," said Jonathan as we continued to walk. "Want to meet me after your breakfast? You could listen to us perform."

"Aren't you afraid? Standing out there in front of those crowds, none of them paying any attention?"

"It's awful sometimes, but it's also wonderful when you see people stop, one by one, and take the time to listen and enjoy."

"Boy, that's really putting yourself on the line."

"It's weird, but I don't feel that way; it's my music I'm taking the chance with, not me, as if we were separate."

"I never thought of it like that. I have trouble separating the two. My music is me. It makes me feel complete." Saying this made me realize how much I missed playing the piano these last months.

"Here I am. Sixty-sixth Street. I have to run. See you later?"

Was it too rushed? Should I hold back? I decided not to get all worried.

"Sure."

"Meet me at 11:30 on the north side of the fountain in front of the Plaza Hotel. We'll check out the scene there before we move downtown." He crossed the street and I heard him shout, "Have a hearty breakfast."

I turned to see if he was looking. He wasn't. With his back still toward me, he waved goodbye over his shoulder. He knew I was watching. That rat! That smug, self-confident . . . and I pictured him shy?

I loved it. I could hardly wait until 11:30.

seven

Aunt Ellen was sitting in a booth in the corner, gazing out on the street through the lace café curtains. She was still wearing her jogging suit.

"Waiting for someone?" I said in a deep voice.

Her head turned. "For you, stranger."

"What a nice place." I stared at the milk-glass vase full of freshly cut daisies.

"It's quiet and soothing."

Violin music trilled in the background.

"How many miles did you run today?"

"Almost three."

"That's good."

"Not great for me. I can do five when I'm in shape. I'm tired. I've been working hard."

"I'm beat, too. I walked from Penn Station."

"Why didn't you take the train?"

"Coming into the city, I met this guy I know from school and walked up with him."

"Beth, I'm glad you're making new friends. It's good for you to get away from the past. What's his name?"

"Jonathan." I was about to burst. I couldn't hold it in. "Aunt Ellen, he's gorgeous. And incredibly talented."

The waitress interrupted to give us menus.

"I know what I'm having," said Aunt Ellen as she handed back the menu. "An herb omelette, a croissant, and cappuccino."

"I'll have the same."

"That's why you look radiant. Tell me more about your young man."

"He's not *my* anything yet!"

She smiled and touched my cheek lovingly.

"Well, he's tall, has blond hair and blue eyes."

"The American Dream. Does he come from a nice family?"

"Who cares? What are you, my mother?"

She stopped and stared.

"I'm sorry; it just came out."

"Give me a break, Beth," and she poked me in the arm.

"Anyway, it's his pants I want to get into."

"That's a switch. Times have changed."

"I'm only kidding."

"Too bad," she joked back.

"Half kidding?"

"You're honest."

"And you're supposed to act like a stodgy maiden aunt and you're not."

"I'll try harder."

"He plays the flute, has a scholarship to Juilliard, and is very bright."

"When am I going to meet him?"

"I just met him officially today. I never spoke to him until this morning. I feel kind of tingly."

"I'm happy for you. It's good to have those feelings inside when a relationship is starting."

"Is that what's happening?" I wouldn't consider what I had with Larry back home a relationship. We talked nightly on the telephone, but sometimes I didn't know why I stayed on the phone with him, except that he was someone to talk to. "A relationship? It sounds so formal, long-lasting. I'm meeting him again in about three hours at the Plaza. He plays music on the street with a group."

"Just enjoy yourself."

The waitress came with our breakfasts.

"I could eat a horse," said Aunt Ellen.

"Me, too."

As we waited for the cappuccino, I asked, "Aunt Ellen, there's something I've been meaning to ask you that I've wondered about for a long time."

"Shoot."

"Why did Mom and Dad get divorced? Was it an affair? With Linda?"

"Oh, nothing like that. Linda was after they separated. And they weren't the types."

"What do you mean, 'the types'?"

"They seemed so much in love. Does that sound crazy? They just couldn't make a go of it over the years. Does that make any sense?"

"Not to me."

"I don't know the whole answer. It's just that many people care for each other deeply, but they can't work out their problems. I see it every day in my office. Who knows what really goes on in people's lives?"

"What do *you* think it was?"

"A combination of things. Marion was always restless. Even as a child. You'd give her a piece of candy, she'd want two. It was never enough. I know she wasn't happy staying at home, being a housewife, homemaker, whatever."

"I hate that. She had me. Couldn't she go on with her life also?"

"She painted, but she never had a showing. Never went to a gallery to present her portfolio and slides of her work. And she was so talented, even in college. She often said, 'I wasted energy over the years.' "

"I don't think raising me was wasted energy. Couldn't she have done her art and taken care of me? Wasn't I an excuse?"

"You're right. Of course, life would have been harder, spending money on baby-sitters and allotting her time."

"Wouldn't she have been happier? She might still be here."

"You don't know that."

"So Mom wanted to do her own thing."

"And she felt she couldn't do it within the marriage. Your father wasn't home to help out. That made matters worse."

"Sometimes she would seethe when Dad came home late, night after night. Maybe she shouldn't have been waiting. Maybe she should have been doing."

"Listen, I don't know if there's an answer. Bob has a demanding profession. When you were young, they didn't have much money."

"Come on. My friend Nance's mother always worked and they still don't have a lot of money. And she's alive. Did *I* need to live in a big house in Westchester? Nance is happy. They all seem to be content in her family."

"Yes. If you want to, you find a way to do it. Some people get sidetracked, unfortunately."

"What turns me off is when I hear people say they can't do this or that because . . . I've got it in me to do my music and there's nothing in the world that can stop me."

"That's wonderful, but not everybody is that way. Your mother had some of that creative drive."

"What did she do with it? Even after Dad was gone?"

Aunt Ellen looked hurt. "You're so hard on her. I remember she called me up a few years ago angry at herself for dreams washed down the drain in loads of laundry. I told her, 'Go back to school for your M.F.A. in painting, get good child care,' but she said, 'How can I apply to a program after being away from school for so long?' I think she was afraid that she was no longer any good. Maybe she was insecure about not being the best. She didn't take the chance of finding out whether she was or not. Your father encouraged her. He said he'd pay for her tuition, which got her even angrier. It accentuated that she wasn't self-sufficient."

"You're telling me it was hard on Mom, and hard on Dad, too."

"I'm not sure of what both of them had to contend with. I do know Bob couldn't stop working. He was willing to contribute in the ways he knew how. I'm not trying to say he was innocent, but neither is he the culprit. I want you to see both sides."

"It's not fair."

"That's right. A no-win situation in their eyes. Life isn't always fair, Beth, but as you've learned, easy things can get complicated when you're dealing with emotions."

"Couldn't it have been worked out?"

"I think the years of frustration were too much for them to handle. People bring extra baggage with them to a marriage."

"What does that mean?"

"It means your mother, your father, many people have unresolved problems which enter into their relationship."

There was that word again.

I asked the waitress what time it was when she put down the check.

"I've got to run," I said. "It's almost eleven."

"Let's do this again. Soon."

"I love you, Aunt Ellen."

"I love you, too."

"Bye."

"Talk to you soon."

"And Beth . . ."

"What?"

"Maybe you should be having this discussion with your father sometime?"

"Ask *him* why they got divorced?"

"Yes, ask him. See his side, too. Think about it."

"I'm not sure."

"Do you feel a little better, now that we've talked?"

"I guess so. Not knowing is worse than knowing."

"For some people."

"For me. I still can't help feeling, wasn't I a good enough reason for Mom to stay around?"

"Of course you were, Beth." And she sighed.

eight

I waited for Jonathan at the fountain in front of the Plaza, pacing around the square. It was 11:15. NO NUKES was sprayed in black on the statue. The graffiti bothered me. How could someone do that? Ruin a piece of art? Even people I agreed with were sometimes idiots. At Hyland North, we made oaktag posters in our E.A.T. club, Energy Alternatives Today, and picketed against nuclear energy for a week. My poster said SUN POWER IS FUN POWER! Poor Mr. Tishman, our principal, popped his bald head out from behind his door every half hour and screamed, "Quiet out here!" and then slammed the door. Mom told me that she had picketed when she was in high school for the right to wear pants, just like the boys, nice dress slacks. The wind whipped up her thighs in the winter. She said that dungarees, which I corrected to jeans, were too risqué then. Mom said issues changed, most people didn't. I hoped that wasn't true. I always wanted to change and grow.

Nance had a self-improvement program for us. We had to choose a bad habit or word we used too often and work to change ourselves. Every week, we picked a new fault. She said that I used too many "Oh, wows!" I got so nervous watching myself, I started saying "Far out" instead, and that was much worse. What drove me crazy about Nance was she picked the cuticles on her nails. We bought a lotion called Bitanail that burned slightly. When she flushed the lotion down the toilet, I informed her she'd never be cast in a Joy liquid commercial. The second week, I said she should stop scratching the mole on her left cheek. "I won't get cancer," she protested. "You don't know what you're talking about." But she stopped doing it.

My feelings were hurt a little when Nance told me I could stand to lose a few pounds. I knew I should, but she didn't have to say it. "Who else should tell you? Svelte Tracey West? Our worst enemy?" Nance was a good friend. She didn't eat any sweets in the cafeteria for a whole week. She lost three pounds. I gained one.

She was so good at thinking up how we could become terrific, I never knew who to expect at homeroom each morning, the old Nance or the new one. I told her she was getting schizy on me and we should cut it out. After four weeks, we got tired and forgot about it. Nance said that she was having an identity crisis. She didn't know who she was any more. It felt better to stagnate for a while.

My thoughts rambled on. Fingers covered my eyes. A mugging! Should I scream or faint? My knees started to wobble. I was about to yell when I heard a familiar voice.

"Hi!" said Jonathan. "Sorry I'm a little late. Come meet my friends."

I saw his group waiting near the hansom cabs lined up around the cobblestone square. Instruments, backpacks, music stands, books, and canvas bags were strewn on the sidewalk. I petted a graceful gray-and-white horse.

"Wan' a ride? Take ya 'round Central Park fer half price," said the driver.

I smiled. "No thanks."

"Sure?"

"Some other time." I felt bolder than I usually did. Ordinarily, I would have ignored him out of fear.

"This is Max, Steve, Charlie, and Yvonne."

"Hi. I'm Beth."

"How do you know the big J?" asked Max.

"We're in the same music-theory class in school."

"That's my man. He's a wiz."

"Don't listen to him," said Jonathan. "He doesn't know what he's saying. Max is lead guitar."

"I've got flying fingers," added Max.

"Charlie's bass. Steve plays the organ. Yvonne is percussion and vocalist."

"Lady drummer," I said mischievously.

"You like that?" asked Max.

"I do."

"So do I." Yvonne gave me a big, toothy smile. I liked her. They all seemed nice.

"Do you play anything?" she asked.

"Yes. The piano, but I'm more into composing."

"Hey, Beethoven," shouted Yvonne to Jonathan, "maybe she could write us something original?"

I felt embarrassed. "I'm not good enough yet."

"Modest," said Charlie, smiling.

"No. I just need more time to develop."

"I'm hip," said Charlie.

"Cool," said Jonathan as he rolled his eyes.

I giggled. "No sweat."

Everyone laughed.

They started taking their instruments out, setting them up to play. Classical, country and Western, bluegrass, rock, punk, and new wave flowed from their instruments during the next two and a half hours. And people stopped. First three teenyboppers, then a young couple holding their baby, an old man with his dog, and more and more, until a crowd formed. People clapped, sang, and danced; others passed by, ignoring them. It was wonderful. And so was Jonathan. He pushed some maracas into my hands. I kept time with them. As I got the beat, my body swayed. Nickels, dimes, and quarters were tossed into an open guitar case. An impeccably dressed gray-haired lady holding a Bergdorf Goodman shopping bag carefully placed down a five-dollar bill with the rest of the loose change, and said, "Keep it up." For a little while, some mimes with painted white faces and black leotards imitated the group as they played. Everyone laughed. Yvonne sang a few songs and Max harmonized. Steve gave Jonathan a sign that he had had it. Yvonne sounded hoarse.

"We did good," said Max, beaming.

"Looks like it," said Steve as he counted the take. "Seventy-five dollars and sixty cents."

"Here's your share," said Jonathan to me.

"What for?"

"You were part of the group."

"No. That's not fair."

Yvonne shoved it into my hand. "Shut up and take it. He isn't always this generous with our money. Play with us next weekend. Bring some of your music." I stood there with the money in my open palm.

"You better close that fist or else someone will think it's a handout," said Jonathan. "Anyone hungry?"

Everyone had somewhere to go. Something to do.

"It's you and me, kid," he said.

I wanted to be alone with him, and I was sort of glad no one could join us. A few hours ago, I had dreaded the thought, but now I looked forward to it. In a coffee shop around the corner, we sat down to juicy cheeseburgers in pita bread.

"You were great," said Jonathan.

"No. You were. I just followed."

We talked about the afternoon in detail, the music and how it went.

The waiter asked, "Can I get you anything else?"

"Not for me. I'm really full."

"I'll pass, too. Just the check, please."

I felt funny about him paying for me. Earlier, he'd said he needed the money. "Let's go Dutch."

He grabbed the check. "I'm not going bankrupt on a hamburger and a Coke. This isn't Lutèce."

Dad took Mom there for her thirtieth birthday. I was only eight then. As she put on her coat, her hair swished and the smell of L'Air du Temps filled the room. She wore a black dress and pearls and looked like a movie star.

Jonathan opened his wallet to pay and something dropped on the floor. I had seen a small package just like it in Nance's older brother's room. We once looked through his drawers for his little black book. Nance wanted to use it as blackmail so he would let her watch Monday Night at the Movies instead of football each week. We never found the book, but we discovered this similar package with all the gory details. Jonathan saw me staring as he bent down to pick it up.

"A memento," he quickly said. "I've been carrying this Trojan for three years."

"You're kidding," I said. "Is it still good? Doesn't it get spoiled or disintegrate like on *Mission: Impossible?*"

"My cousin Henry had some for five years before he used them, and no bad reports. He said he checked for holes by blowing them up first like balloons. What a clown. I knew he was wrong, but I didn't want to embarrass him."

"Oh," I said, looking at the flecks on the tiled floor.

Jonathan continued. "My Uncle Morty gave it to me at my Bar Mitzvah. He shoved it in my hand and chuckled like a dirty old man. 'Use this and then you can say, today I am a man!' "

"That's gross!"

"Yeah. Mom would have been annoyed if she knew about the bag and that her brother Morty isn't a class act, but he means well. My Aunt Miriam, Morty's wife, put an announcement about the Bar Mitzvah in her Hadassah magazine."

"I don't see my family much," I said. "Just my Aunt Ellen. She's terrific. She's almost like a close friend."

"Is she your mother or father's sister?"

"My mother's."

I thought, *"Was* my mother's." Everything became blurred in the coffee shop, but there was no way I was going to cry right there.

"You look far-off. Anything wrong?"

"My mother is dead."

"I'm sorry."

"You have nothing to be sorry about. People always say that. It wasn't your fault. You didn't even know her."

"Hey, I'm sorry for *you*, Beth."

I liked the way he said my name. I looked into his eyes. His pupils were rimmed with yellow. Orange spokes radiated outward like a bicycle wheel through his gray-blue eyes. He reached for my hand as we got up to leave.

"It's so easy talking to you, Jonathan."

"You're silly." He pulled me gently toward him, and stroked my hair. We stood outside in the cool evening air. I didn't mind him holding me in public. I felt protected from the world. "This is our first date." He looked down at me, smiling. It felt right.

"Let's get a chocolate chocolate-chip cone," he said. "Down the block on the way to Penn Station."

"My treat. You paid for the meal."

"You are one liberated woman."

I liked that. No one had called me a woman before.

Jonathan got a hot-fudge macadamia-nut sundae after he finished his double-scoop cone. I got myself a mocha-chip cone. One scoop. I paid for it with the nickels and dimes and quarters we had gotten that afternoon.

"We really pigged-out," said Jonathan, smiling.

"We?!!" I shouted.

Neon signs lit up the darkness as we walked along, eating and talking. I thought about the Trojan as we passed a pharmacy. I wondered if Jonathan had done it yet? And if I'd find out?

"Beth, I really want to hear what you've written."

"Oh, Jonathan. I don't know."

"Come on. Take a chance."

"Well . . ." I thought about my mother. Wasn't not taking chances what she was about?

"This Wednesday night? I'll come over?"

"I don't have a piano." Besides, I didn't want him at Dad's house. With Linda. And questions.

"Well, my house? My parents wouldn't mind. And I told you already that my mom has a piano."

I hadn't played in a couple of months, since I'd been out of school, and Grandma's old piano was in storage.

"What kind of piano?" I asked.

"I've got you," he said. "Where do you live?"

I gave him my address.

"It's not a long walk to my house, or you could take your bike."

"Let me think about it." I wanted to see Jonathan, but I wasn't sure if I wanted him, of all people, to hear my music.

"Let's make it Wednesday. Potluck night. You'll come for dinner."

He was so casual. Linda would have needed a printed invitation, black tie, R.S.V.P., and the linen tablecloth.

"Okay. Wednesday. You wore me down."

"Starve yourself. My mother's a good cook."

So was mine.

nine

Jonathan called me Monday night.

"Did you cut music today?"

"No. I wasn't in school."

"Are you okay?"

"I'm sick. I have a bad cold and was in bed all day yesterday."

"You sound kind of distant."

"I'm all stuffed up."

"Can I do anything?"

"Thanks. All I need is sleep, hot tea with lemon and honey, and my mother's chicken soup."

I missed my mother waiting on me hand and foot. When I was sick, I could count on her to be Florence Nightingale. Every day, she stripped the sheets off my bed and aired them out the window, where they blew in the wind like flags. Crawling between sheets that were cool and smooth, not damp and crumpled, made me feel fifty percent better. I would slide under the covers, tucking the blanket up to my nose, falling peacefully into a drugged sleep. Waking to the smell of my mother's soup wafting up from the kitchen, I knew I was on my way back from the grave.

"Listen, I don't think I'll be able to make it this Wednesday."

"See how you are."

"I'm just letting you know. I don't want to hang your mother up."

"It's another mouth. I have two other sisters and brothers."

"My God, five kids! Didn't your parents ever hear of birth control? You certainly have."

"Hey. Watch your step." He teased me back. "They either wanted a large family or it's because my mother was religious when they first got married."

"What does that mean?"

"She was an Orthodox Jew and not too keen on contraception."

"Oh, like us, we're Catholic."

"You're Catholic and your mother made chicken soup?"

"Jonathan, chickens aren't Jewish."

"They're not?"

"Come on."

"I'll call you. I hope you can come over."

"Me, too."

On Wednesday, I was still home from school and I knew that I'd never be able to see Jonathan for dinner. The cold had settled in my chest. When I coughed, I sounded like a truck screeching to a halt.

"Take these." Linda handed me two aspirins, a 500-milligram tablet of vitamin C, and a brown bottle filled with a greenish liquid. One whiff and I knew it was the cough syrup that gave me the shudders. I gulped down the pills, not leaving any water for the medicine.

"Bob, Beth needs more water. Could you get it? While you're up, a spoon too." Lisa woke up from her late-afternoon nap wailing with hunger. It was way past dinner time. Linda ran out of my room, pushing the bottle into my father's free hand as he entered.

"This gunk is disgusting. I'm not taking any." Thinking about the syrup going down my throat sent chills through my body.

Dad easily untwisted the cap that I had tried to tighten with all my strength, and licked the top of the bottle just like when I was a kid. "Not bad. Close your eyes and hold your nose, and you won't taste the medicine."

"You can't pull that one off on me any more."

"Try it. Trust me."

Since I wanted to get well and see Jonathan, I did what Dad told me to.

"Now that wasn't so bad?"

"It was the pits."

"I'll be back in four hours with a second dose."

"Yes, doctor."

Linda cut us off. She screamed up the stairs, "Beth, pick up the phone!"

"Hi," I said in a raspy voice.

"Is this Bela Lugosi? This is Jonathan Schein."

"I sound terrible, don't I?"

"Yeah. But how do you look?"

"The same way I sound. Why?"

"Because I'm coming over."

"Oh no you're not. You'll get sick." I wasn't going to let him see me like this.

"Vanity, thy name is woman."

"Male chauvinist pig!"

"Remember, I'm kosher. See you in ten minutes."

"Ten minutes. I'm going to kill you!"

As soon as I finished washing my face and brushing my hair, the doorbell rang.

"I'll get it." I threw my hairbrush on the gold-speckled Formica counter top, and started down the hall.

"Stay where you are. You'll get a draft," said Linda.

"Who could that be?" questioned my father as he followed Linda out of their room.

I stood at the top of the stairs in the hallway and watched the interrogation.

"Hello. I'm Jonathan Schein, Beth's friend from school."

My father shook Jonathan's already extended hand.

"This is my wife, Linda."

"And this is Lisa." Linda held her up to her cheek.

"Come in," said Dad.

All three of them sat on the couch facing Jonathan, who remained standing.

"Sit down." Dad patted the arm of the club chair.

"Well, I really came over to give Beth her music homework."

"Wouldn't it have been easier over the phone?" asked Linda.

"I needed to show her a few things."

"I hope you don't catch her cold." Linda coughed. "I pray I don't. That's all I need."

"Don't worry, Mr. and Mrs. Corey, I'll take the chance."

My father tensed. "Talking about taking chances, Beth mentioned she met a friend who plays music on the street in Manhattan. Is that you?"

"Yes. It's me."

I decided to intervene, sick or not, draft or not. "Hi, Jonathan, what are you doing here?" I asked.

"You'd better get upstairs before you get sicker," said Linda, eyeing me in my bathrobe.

"I don't want Beth playing any music on the street," Dad continued, "or even standing around watching. It attracts all types." He was oblivious to me.

"What types, Mr. Corey?"

"People who take drugs, derelicts. I don't want Beth there."

I came to Jonathan's defense. And mine. "A well-dressed lady with a Bergdorf Goodman shopping bag gave us five dollars. Which category does she fit?"

"Five dollars! That's begging, as far as I'm concerned. If you both like music so much, go to the New York Philharmonic."

"Jonathan and I could never afford that, Dad!"

"I'll pay for the tickets."

"Mr. Corey, I don't want you paying for our tickets. I do odd jobs, help out Mr. Gardini's Landscaping Service once in a while, and play my music on the street for extra money, and also because I want to *play* my music."

Dad turned toward me. "Linda and I discussed it and she feels the same way."

"There are free concerts at the band shell in town, or at the church or the library," said Linda.

That did it. Who the hell was Linda to decide what I should do?

"Let's go up to my room, Jonathan."

"You can go into the den," said Dad.

"It's all right. I'll leave the door open."

Jonathan shrugged his shoulders and smiled. His eyes met my father's.

"She's my little girl," he said.

"Lisa is your *little* girl." And I ran up the steps.

"Wow, am I angry!" I said, slamming the door to my bedroom.

"Don't you think we should leave it open?"

"I don't care. What are we going to do, anyway, with all of them downstairs?"

"Well," said Jonathan, raising his eyebrows up and down. "You gorgeous creature, get over here."

In the oval mirror above my dresser I noticed two raw nostrils staring at me.

"You must be nuts. Look at me! Rudolph the Red-nosed Reindeer reincarnated."

"You didn't know I have a thing about reindeer."

"You're crazy." I jumped in my bed and hid under the covers, pretending not to breathe.

"Ah, to think the princess fell into a deep sleep before receiving my gift."

"What gift?" I popped my head over the top of the blanket. "What gift? Where?" I repeated.

"Oh, nothing." He looked innocently at the ceiling, tapping his foot lightly on the floor, while he sat at the edge of my bed.

I poked my hands under his jacket as he hid his hands behind his back. His shirt was moist near the small of his back.

"Aggressive, aren't you? Now I know why you closed the door."

"Jonathan!"

"She wants my body!"

We tickled each other until we both hurt so much from laughing we had to stop. I hoped no one heard downstairs. I was doubled over. So was Jonathan. After minutes passed, breathlessly, Jonathan handed me a brown-paper frozen-food bag tied with a purple ribbon.

"What's this?"

"Open it."

Inside the bag was a white plastic tub filled with a wobbling gelatinous yellow blob.

"What is it?"

"A sad story. My cousin Henry, the one I told

you about. The family has kept it a secret for years. It's one of those rare, degenerative diseases, possibly hereditary, poor thing, and this is all that's left of him. Actually, my theory is it's what his last date reduced him to."

"Well, hello, Henry. You look pretty good, considering."

"He's in the last stage of his illness. He's suffered so," he whispered. "Seriously, this is my grandmother's one and only special recipe for chicken soup, with matzo balls."

"I'd never have guessed." I feigned shock.

"My grandma's *knedlach*, that's what she calls them, anchor to the bottom of the soup bowl. You can imagine what they do to the stomach. Bowling balls. When I was five, my mother thought I needed an appendectomy because of my writhing on the floor. 'Such an actor,' Mama would say. My mother makes it better than Mama does. Her matzo balls float on top of the soup."

"My mom made her soup with thick noodles." I put my hand to my clammy forehead, not wanting Jonathan to see my change of mood.

"Don't, Beth. I wanted to make you feel better, not worse."

"I know. You're really something."

"What?"

"Something special."

He put his hands on my shoulders.

It started drizzling, and I thought of the first time I had seen him doing the lawn. A spider was weaving its web outside the window. The web glistened in the light from the street below. A bug was caught, trying to escape.

"What's wrong, Beth?"

"I don't know."

And he held me, knowing not to ask any more questions.

There was a knock at the door.

"Is everything all right?"

I opened it. "Yes, Dad. Everything is fine."

Even though everything wasn't.

ten

I had really done it to myself this time. I was a basket case from my bad cold. One good thing happened. The three pounds I had always tried to lose when I dieted along with Nance disappeared.

Jonathan and I talked on the phone every night. One afternoon after school, he dropped off a piece of music for me to look over while I was still sick in bed. It was hard for me to imagine without a piano how I'd play it, but I tried to see how it sounded. I was very excited to try it out. Prokofiev's Sonata for Flute and Piano in D major, Opus 94. For piano and flute only. A duet.

A week later, I finally returned to school, still feeling under the weather because of my cough. During study hall, Jonathan and I had permission from

Mr. Wheldon to use one of the rehearsal rooms downstairs in the basement. I peered through a small glass window framed in a door and saw a girl playing the violin while another girl, whose cello looked bigger than she was, waited for her cue. All this quiet was so strange because if I opened just one door, sound would pour out into the long, narrow corridor.

Jonathan was already practicing when I got to room 035. Peter, a boy from our theory class, was there. My disappointment faded when he handed Jonathan some books and left.

"Hi. You made it down to the dungeon."

"It's spooky in this basement, but I kind of like it."

"Quieter than the cafeteria. What a zoo!"

"Or study hall."

"Sorry I left you there, but I had to run to the office. My sister Rachel wasn't feeling well, so I called my mom at work."

"Is she okay?"

"Yeah. I guess a bug's going around. Are you ready?" he asked, flattening out the pages of his music.

"I haven't actually played my part yet."

"Take your time, I'll be back in fifteen minutes. Be just down the hall."

I struggled with the first few bars, but didn't rush it. Go slow. Concentrate. Stumbling through two pages, over and over, the fifteen minutes didn't seem long enough. I wasn't used to sight-reading after being away from it for two months, but I knew it would come back.

"Ready now?"

I looked up and sighed.

"Come on. We don't have to go through the whole piece, but you've got to start somewhere."

"There's a first time for everything, right?"

"That's right."

And we both grinned.

Half an hour later, the buzzer rang to change classes. When Jonathan turned off the light and put his hand on the back of my neck, my stomach did a flip. After he locked the door, he bent down and kissed me. I liked his lips on mine and the sound of his breathing. I kissed him back before the other students rushed into the hallway from their cubbyholes with instruments banging about.

"See you at three?" he asked.

"I'll be a little late. I have to take a make-up test for trigonometry."

"Enjoy yourself."

"Thanks a lot. At three-thirty?"

"Sure. I'll be on the front lawn."

"If I pass, we'll celebrate. Banana splits on me!"

"It's a deal. Good luck."

At a quarter to four, I dragged myself out the front doors of Bleeker. Jonathan was waiting.

"Thanks for staying, the test was a killer."

"I figured as much when you didn't show up on time. Did you pass?"

"Who knows?"

"Now you really need that banana split just to revive yourself."

We walked down the street and into the pink and brown store.

"I'm still treating."

"Good, because looking through my back pockets about ten minutes ago, I realized I'm down to my last eighty cents."

"Do you need any money? For the bus, at least?"

"No, thanks. I'll work in my father's dry-cleaning store in Queens after school tomorrow; I get out of classes early. Could you come this Wednesday?"

"Not this Wednesday. There are tryouts for the June graduation recital. I've got to brush up on my Rachmaninoff piece as much as I can. I'm going to stay late every day after school until next Tuesday."

"Out of practice?"

"You heard that I was, to put it mildly. Are you trying out?"

"No. I'm in it. I've been rehearsing a piece with Mr. Wheldon since March."

"Show-off."

"Listen, I can't help it if I was the boy genius who won the scholarship to Juilliard."

"Modest, too."

"That's what happens if you've been playing since you're six."

"Beat you. I began the piano at five."

"Show-off."

"Hey. That's my line."

"Then next Wednesday."

"Next Wednesday," I said.

When we were done with our ice cream, we caught the bus on Main Street. Until he reached his stop, I rested my hand on his thigh as he held my hand, feeling content to say nothing.

I practiced for almost three hours every day after school until Tuesday. Jonathan said I could come over on the weekend to his house and use his mother's piano, but I felt funny. Tuesday night, he called to see how it went, and I told him the good news. Mr. Wheldon said he'd be posting the final announcements on Wednesday, but he whispered to me that I played beautifully, and he'd leave a place for me in June's program. Jonathan gave a walloping shout at the other end of the phone. Linda looked at me strangely as she passed by, overhearing Jonathan's enthusiasm. He said he'd see me tomorrow night and he'd ask his mother to think up something special. We made up I would come over early.

The following afternoon, I finished my homework at around four-thirty and went downstairs to tell Linda. She was reading to Lisa in such an animated voice, she seemed a different person. Lisa was trying to turn the pages to see the pictures.

"Baba," she mouthed.

"Bow-wow. Doggy." Linda pointed to the picture.

I moved closer, observing an exquisitely detailed illustration of a dog holding a black leather bag in its mouth. Linda continued. I didn't hear the words. A long time had passed since my parents cuddled me in a chair to tell a story. Linda leaned the book on her lap and looked up.

"Yes, Beth?" Her finger remained on her last sentence.

"I won't be here for dinner tonight. I was invited to go to Jonathan's."

"Do you feel well enough? You're sneezing a lot, still."

"I'm better."

"Where does he live? Do you need a ride?"

"No. I'll walk. It's not far."

"Don't get sweated up. You'll get a draft. You don't want a relapse, do you?"

Linda and her drafts.

"Leave his telephone number. Don't be home too late. When you come in, please don't slam the front door and be quiet on the steps. I don't want Lisa waking up."

"I'll slither like a snake under the door past Lisa's room into mine."

"That's not what I meant. Just be considerate."

"I am."

"Well then . . . Oh, Beth, do we have to go through this all the time?"

"Have to go through what?"

"Nothing," she sighed. "It's late in the afternoon and I'm too tired. Just be home early." Linda nuzzled Lisa, who was getting fidgety, and continued to read.

It was already May, and finally I was going to Jonathan's house for dinner. He lived on a hill past the Duck Pond on a dead-end street in a dark-brown-shingled house. Perched on an anemic lawn was a rusty mailbox with the name *Schein* scrolled on it. It was the smallest house on the block. Where did all his sisters and brothers sleep? In bunk beds? Like sardines? A single star and a half-moon were carved in each red shutter. Flakes of old dried paint hung from the gutters on the narrow front porch. Weeds grew between the cracks in the cement path.

As I rang the doorbell, the wooden slats of the porch creaked beneath me. I thumped a brass knocker on the front door when no one came. Finally, a boy about seven years old looked through the locked screen door.

"Could you tell your brother Beth is here?"

"Ma-a-a, there's a girl here for Jonathan."

His mother came to the door in her apron, patting her hair with her fingers. "Hello. We've been expecting you. Jonathan must be upstairs listening to his tapes. He never hears the bell, or anything for that matter, when he's engrossed in his music. Sorry David left you standing out here alone, but he's been told not to let strangers in."

"He did the right thing, then."

Mrs. Schein had dark, olive skin and shiny black hair that she wore in a pageboy. And Jonathan's smile. Her green eyes twinkled when she spoke, just like his. She was about five feet three inches, had a small frame, like me, and a nice figure. I couldn't believe she'd had five children.

"I'm Beth Corey. I recently moved to Bayview."

"I know. Come into the kitchen with me." She touched the side of my arm gently. "I was in the midst of making the salad. Jonathan is doing his homework. I can tell because Rampal is on. He only plays classical flute when he's doing his assignments." She waved her arm in the air above her head in exasperation. "It drives his father nuts. 'How can he do two things at once? Study and absorb anything with music on?' But Jonathan gets high grades. To tell you the truth, it baffles me, too. I don't know how he does it."

"Neither do I." I smiled. "I need everything extremely quiet. I crammed for the Regents in the bathroom, running the bathtub faucet. The sound of the water blotted out any other noise."

"Like a Japanese garden. I love the water slowly trickling over the stones."

"More like Niagara Falls."

"Your parents must have some water bill."

"My mother did complain. She and my father were divorced. Now she's gone."

"Gone?"

"Dead." Why did I feel the need to tell her that? I was annoyed at myself.

"I see. Jonathan mentioned you were living with your father and his wife."

"And their baby," I added.

"Yes. And your stepsister. I forgot."

I never thought of Lisa being related, and nothing as close as a sister.

"Can I help with anything?" I changed the subject.

"You could finish the salad."

I sliced tomatoes and cucumbers on a large cutting board into a wooden salad bowl. Mom and I liked to cook together.

"Do you like oil-and-vinegar dressing? We're having Italian food. I could eat it every day!"

"I love Italian food. Oil-and-vinegar is fine, Mrs. Schein."

"Rochelle. My name's Rochelle. The tape's off. Could you do me a favor and tell Jonathan to come down and prepare the garlic bread. That's his department. I hate peeling all those cloves, chopping them into tiny specks. Jonathan is my garlic press. I'll have to start working on Michael. He's next in line. Before I look around, Jonathan will be off to college. And if Michael doesn't want to fill the task, my destiny is Woolworth's housewares."

Mom used to love going to the Cellar at Macy's or to Bloomingdale's just to browse in the housewares department. She knew every piece of gourmet equipment: Cuisinart, quiche pans, snail-shell prongs for escargots. She could spend days there. Natural-straw placemats, country French tablecloths with peasant designs, Irish linen napkins, it was endless. And then she'd come home with truffles or a dozen brioches. Mom dreamed of being locked in overnight. She would have looked like a beached whale by the morning if that ever happened. I'm positive if they pumped her stomach they would have found an entire tin of Droste's chocolate coffee beans had been consumed.

I went upstairs, hesitating at the landing. An Eric Clapton album was now playing. I passed Mr. and Mrs. Schein's small bedroom. I paused at the doorway of the boys' room opposite theirs. It looked like Pete's Pet Paradise, my old haunt when I was that age and owned a Dutch rabbit. How did they sleep with all those smells from gerbils, hamsters, turtles, and fish?

The next room was right out of *Seventeen* magazine. Matching everything, home sewn. A poster of John Travolta was on the back of an open closet door and a Miss Piggy calendar was on the corkboard.

Then I stood at the threshold of Jonathan's room. It was the size of a large closet, looking cluttered and lived in. Three rows of bookcases above the bed over his head looked as if they could fall any minute from the weight of all the junk, squashing Jonathan, who was stretched out on his stomach, reading a book.

"What are you reading?"

He jumped up and banged his head on the lowest shelf. "You could give a guy a heart attack. I'm reading a new sci-fi, *It Happened in Kansas,* creatures from other planets landing in cornfields, the whole bit."

"Sorry. I came up to tell you to make the garlic bread."

"How long have you been here?"

"About twenty minutes."

"I was finishing my homework. I didn't hear you."

"I know. Rampal was on."

"I guess you met my mom, then."

"She's great."

"Yeah. She's flaky sometimes. On a scale of one to ten, my mother's an eight and three-quarters."

"What happened to the other one and a quarter?"

"Parents don't get full rating."

"I'll have to remember never to have children."

"You'd get a ten."

"Boy, I must rate." I gave him a playful punch in the stomach and said, "Last one down is a rotten egg." I could hear him running behind me.

"Where's the fire?" asked Mrs. Schein.

"In my heart, Mother."

"Oh, God, he's still my most dramatic child. The first always is. He got all my attention for over two years."

"Until the rest of the mob came along. Then I was neglected and abused."

"Very underprivileged. Here's the garlic. Chop. Make yourself useful. If you're going to play a role in a Dickens novel, I'll play one, too. A female Fagin."

Mrs. Schein rolled her fingers in the air like Fagin did in *Oliver Twist* and we all laughed.

I heard footsteps scampering on the front porch and a bicycle crashing to the pavement. "Ma, Dad's home." It sounded like David's voice. In walked a tall man, muscular, with blond graying hair.

"Hi, honey. Stopped by Umberto's Fish Market. These were on sale."

She unwrapped what seemed like a bushel of clams. "They look so fresh, Sol."

"I know what's for dinner now. Chop more garlic," mimicked Jonathan. "Dad, this is Beth Corey. She's staying for dinner."

"Hello. Hope you like clams and linguine."

"I do, Mr. Schein."

"I'll be back down to help with the meal. I want to get washed up and unwind." He kissed Mrs.

Schein on the cheek and she smiled. "Where are the girls?"

"Kerin is baby-sitting. Rachel is studying at the library. They should be home very soon." Mrs. Schein handed some brushes and a bowl full of clams to Michael and David. "Start scrubbing those shells. Wash your hands first."

"Ugh. Do we have to? Can't we make the salad?" asked Michael.

"It's already made. Beth and I did it."

"How about the dessert? I could buy ice cream."

She shot him a look. "That takes a lot of effort. Scrub, guys, or no dinner tonight for us all."

"I wasn't hungry, anyway," whined David.

"Listen, squirt," said Jonathan, "you know clams are your favorite, so who are you kidding? He'll eat them fried, chopped, baked, or stuffed. Nice Jewish boy? I didn't even know from clams at his age."

I heard loud giggling and the sound of roller skates on the cement sidewalk outside the kitchen window.

"That must be the girls." Mrs. Schein hugged the younger one as she came in.

"Hi, Mom." The older one grabbed a carrot and munched.

"Dad's home. Wash up and cut these vegetables."

"All we do is work!" Kerin pouted.

"I never saw such an uncooperative bunch." Mrs. Schein winked and smiled at me.

"Rachel, Kerin, this is Beth, Jonathan's friend."

Kerin started giggling and covered her braces with her hand. She looked like Mrs. Schein. It was amazing the way the kids came out looking like their parents. Rachel was tall and blond like Jonathan and Mr. Schein. Her eyes were blue, unlike Kerin's and Michael's; theirs were green like Mrs. Schein's. It was really weird that they were all one family, like Mendel's peas we had studied in biology. And little David was a hybrid of them both. People told me I looked like a clone of my mother. I didn't see the resemblance.

"Hi, Beth. You in Jonathan's class?" asked Rachel.

"Yes. Music theory."

"Is the teacher Mr. Wheldon? I have him for music appreciation. I'm a freshman at Bleeker."

"Jailbait," teased Jonathan.

Rachel tried to sock him in the arm. As they raced around the kitchen table, Jonathan fended her off by whipping a dish towel at her knees.

"Ma," screamed Rachel.

"That's enough!" yelled Mrs. Schein as the others tried to get into the action. "I'm looking forward to when I'm sixty and you're all married."

"Just in time for grandchildren." Jonathan laughed.

"What's going on?" asked Mr. Schein as he came in, looking relaxed in jeans and a polo shirt.

"The usual nonsense," said Mrs. Schein.

"So what can I do?"

"Sit down at the table."

"No, really?"

"Rinse this pot, boil up the water, slice these lemons, and open the wine."

"Should I put the extension in the dining-room table?"

"No. We'll eat in the kitchen. It's a little more crammed, but I don't feel formal tonight. Kerin, please set the table."

Linda would never have people over to eat in the kitchen. But this was warm and cozy. I felt as if I were home again. I chopped and peeled the garlic with Jonathan. There was something nice about the noise of this large family.

After we cleared some of the dishes, Jonathan took me by the hand, led me into the living room, and we sat down on the piano bench. "Did you bring your music?"

"Yes," I said reluctantly.

"Well, then?"

"Now?"

"Do you know a better time?"

I went upstairs to his room to get the composition I had left in my purse, and went to the bathroom before I came back down. The palms of my hands were sweating just like at my piano recitals when I was little. I washed and dried them on a towel. Returning, I slid between the bench and the piano, carefully positioning myself in the center, and rested my foot near the damper pedal.

"Do you need me to turn the pages?" he asked.

"No, thanks. I can do it myself."

Jonathan sat behind me in an armchair, so I couldn't see his reaction while I was playing. Thank

God. I began to play. It was me and my music. I was no longer playing for him. It seemed no one else was in the room any more. All that was important was the feeling. When I stopped, it was so silent that Mrs. Schein startled me when she walked in from the kitchen.

"You play very nicely. Now let's have dessert."

Her hand was on my long hair. For an instant, it seemed like my mother's. I turned around and hugged her. I was surprised I did that. But I did. She didn't even question it. She hugged me back.

"You're very good," said Mr. Schein as he touched my shoulder and his wife's.

"I'm okay. It needs work."

"Everything always needs work. Nothing is ever really finished. Maybe that's why we all go on?" said Mrs. Schein, slipping her arm around my waist. "You're very good." She repeated Mr. Schein's words with an air of finality, so I accepted what she said.

"My parents like you," said Jonathan.

"I like them, too," I said, staring off at the twinkling sky as Jonathan walked me home. The water of the bay blended with the horizon. Only specks of light from the docked boats and seafood restaurants dotted the blackness like a magical collage suspended in midair.

"A penny for your thoughts?" he asked.

"You didn't tell me what *you* think of my music."

"Wasn't it obvious?"

"I want to hear it from you."

"Hmm." He paused. "You're terrific. I think you could be a composer someday."

"I'm not now?"

"I mean famous, respected, renowned."

"If only," I sighed.

"It can happen. Anything can happen with persistence if you've got the talent. And the luck. All you'll need is your first break. Then you'll do it."

"Do you really think so?"

"There are some things you feel in your guts. And that's the way we feel about music. It's part of our flesh and blood. We need it like the air to breathe. And when you feel that way about something, it's got to happen if you work hard enough."

"Do you believe that? I wish I had your confidence."

"Stop putting yourself down. Why don't you?"

"Because I don't."

"Why are you so held back in certain ways and in others you're so direct?"

"Like?"

"Like now, you can't enjoy praise about your music."

"And?"

"And you hugged my mother, which floored me. Sometimes I think I know where you're at, and then you flip to something unexpected."

"It's because I don't know what I want at times. Especially lately."

"That's normal."

"No. It's more than that. I have something to

tell you. Jonathan, my mother killed herself. That's how she really died."

He stopped walking. We were a block away from my house.

"My mom overdosed on sleeping pills. I found her." The words stuck in my throat. "The last four months have been awful."

"Beth, that's horrible."

"I feel guilty, angry. You name it. Sometimes I don't feel at all. Just numb. I wish she'd died of cancer. You know what I mean? It's as if my mother isn't alive and she isn't dead. All those unanswered questions I can't put to rest. I never want attachments like I had with her."

"Not even to me?" asked Jonathan.

I half smiled back. "Well . . ."

"I don't know what to say," said Jonathan. "No one has ever told me anything like this before."

"There's nothing you can say, really."

Holding hands, we continued to walk, until we reached the front door. He leaned over to kiss me.

"I hope I didn't taste like garlic," I whispered.

"See you tomorrow," he said. "You're funny."

And he gave me another long kiss.

eleven

She killed herself. There, I said it. Where is the pain? The tears? Emotions you're supposed to feel. I haven't cried. I can't cry. What's wrong with me? Does it mean I didn't love her? How could someone not love her own mother? I'm angry at her for leaving me. Alone with Dad. Alone with Linda. Alone with their baby. Alone in the world.

If she loved me, really loved me, and cared, would she have left me that way? She knew how I felt about Linda and Dad. She didn't like them, either. There should be a rule made somewhere that mothers can never be selfish. Didn't she love me enough to think of what would happen to me? I hate her for only caring about herself.

She came into my room the night before I found her. The only light came from the flickering television in her bedroom. The sound was off. In the dark, she sat on my bed, smoothed the sheet over and over, and whispered, "Beth, you're a strong person. You have inner strength. You might look small and fragile, but underneath you're tough. I know you'll get by."

I didn't want to get by. I wanted more. Much more. "What's up?" I asked her.

She kissed me on the forehead, rubbed her finger lightly across my cheekbone, and smiled. The sleeve of her flannel nightgown brushed against my face and felt like peach skin. Her breath smelled minty, of toothpaste. I thought to myself, it's a mood. We all have our moods. She didn't seem out of it, just very serene. Bland. When I think about it now, she must have been very troubled to have come into my room late at night and blurt that out. Why couldn't she talk? Open up to me? Let me help her? There I go again. Me being the mother, she being the child. She put me in that role for so long. It was the little things, but it was the little things that got to me, that made me feel I was spoon-fed responsibility. She'd have me borrow milk from a neighbor I disliked, return spoiled cottage cheese to the manager at the superette, call up the operator for information because she said they sounded too authoritarian, or try to exchange a blouse that was marked "Final Sale." I can hear her laughing. "You're so mature, Beth, you should bring me up!" At ten, I thought it was funny. At sixteen, I didn't think it was a joke. Where was my childhood? When was it? In the past, if ever. Did it leave with Dad when he left six years ago, or was it long before that?

Mom missed him after he left. In her heart, I don't think she wanted to separate. She never said anything. I know she was surprised when Dad said that he wanted a divorce. How could two people live together and not know the other one was unhappy? But then look at me. Didn't I live with Mom? Maybe I was too busy with all the after-school stuff that everyone did so it got listed on your high-school record and looked good when you finally applied to college: music lessons, reporter on the school newspaper, jogging team, and solar-energy club. There was the French summer exchange program, which indicated fluency in another language; actually, I baked in the sun for two months. I spent time away at riding academies, weight-reduction and tennis camps, being molded for something perfect and successful, not too unlike my father. Dad said he loved me. And in a way he'd always love Mom, too, but he just couldn't live with her. Could you love someone and not want to be with them? I loved Mom. And I loved Dad. I wanted to see them both. Tell them when I got an A on a test, made a new friend, or conquered a Bach fugue.

The first few months after the divorce, my mother sometimes wandered from room to room. A cup of tea tilted in her hand, she'd stare out the living-room window, as if she expected Dad's car to turn into the graveled driveway after one of his late-night meetings. The moonlight would glow through her nightgown, showing off her figure. It was strange to watch, and very painful.

I woke up once and heard the TV. It was 12:45 a.m. Barely awake, I drifted into Mom's room, thinking that she had fallen asleep with it on. The remote control was next to her. She was sitting on her bed doing her toenails in ruby red. Mom was not a colored-toenail person. "The movie's that good?" My eyes blinked from the brightness in the middle of the pitch-black room. "One of those old Bette Davis ones, I eat them up." She continued to do her nails.

"Do you want some hot cocoa from scratch?" I asked. "With crackers and cream cheese?"

"That would be a real treat." She smiled like a child who had been given a birthday gift early. We cuddled in bed together as we watched Bette. The cocoa warmed our insides. The crumbs got on the blanket. Mom didn't care. We touched toes to keep warm. It was a cold night. There was a time when I was small enough to fit my body into the curl of hers. Now I think about Mom gazing emptily at the television and how very lonely it must have been for her.

Aunt Ellen told Mom she had to get back into the mainstream of life. Date. Work. She went out to dinner with her friends, dated occasionally, but no one was good enough for her. "After twelve years of marriage, I'm not good at dating," she said. "It means smiling a lot, being pleasant. I'd rather stay at home reading a good book than sharing my thoughts and spending my time with someone in a supposedly meaningful evening." Aunt Ellen said that she didn't believe her. She felt that she was frightened. I thought it was fun watching her get dressed up, and I was old enough to stay at home without a baby-sitter. The next day, she'd describe to me where she had been, and what she had done, even if it was just a movie. Finally, Mom realized Dad wasn't going to come back; he had already married Linda by the time I was thirteen. There was a secret part of me that always hoped he would come home again.

At the art gallery in town, Mom's most recent job, she'd met a nice man. He came over for lunch one Sunday, and I liked him. I told Mom he was cute. We played Chinese checkers and poker all afternoon. And I won. After a while, my mother stopped seeing him. She said that he didn't fulfill her needs emotionally, and the job didn't intellectually. Or was it the other way around?

The day I found her, I had shouted my usual, "Bye, Mom. See you later." I was late for the bus, and I was having an audition that morning for the school orchestra. She was usually up by this time, brewing one of her herb teas. She was still. I thought she had taken a sleeping pill the night before. Sometimes she'd do that. I'd say, "Ma, why are you taking those?" as she leaned over the sink, casually plucking her eyebrows.

"It's no big deal, honey. I have a full day tomorrow and I need my rest, a real good night's sleep."

"I don't understand how someone who eats health foods could put that junk into their body."

She grinned. "You're right, what can I say? I don't want to have to think when I put my head down on that pillow. I want to sleep." Then she'd kiss me good night.

I left without hearing her say back sleepily, "See you later, alligator." Halfway to the bus, I turned around and came back, thinking I should take the Haydn piece I had been practicing all week. The house was too quiet. It didn't feel right. Why I felt this way, I will never know. Was I still connected to my mother? The window was open, the white organdy curtains were blowing. The sunlight cast shadows on her face. Her mouth hung open, saliva was dripping on the pillow. She had changed the sheets and cases the day before. There was a stillness in her bedroom, like a lake in the early-morning sunrise.

"Mom, are you asleep?" I leaned over.

"Hey, Mom?" I nudged her. "Are you okay? Ma!"

I started shaking her. She didn't move. I froze and stared at my mother curled up like a baby. She wasn't breathing. In a panic, I ran out of the room, forgetting there was a phone right next to her bed. I raced downstairs. Away. I called Aunt Ellen. And then Dad. Linda answered. I couldn't tell her. I didn't want to talk to her. Dad had already left for work. I knew that. I don't know why I called. I hung up. Later on, I found the Haydn piece in my book bag between my math and English homework.

I dreamed for weeks of walking endlessly down a long, narrow bridge with dark gray-blue water on either side. A pale slate mist enveloped me. I felt scared and helpless. Silently, I mourned my mother as I slept. In the middle of the night, I'd sit up, startled. Each morning, the sheet and blanket soaked, my hair wet and stringy, perspiration dripping down my neck, I'd open my eyes and then what had happened hit me. My mother's suicide was real. It wasn't a dream.

Sleep lasted a long time. When I was awake, it was a half sleep. My mother would never see the sun rise again, inhale the morning air, eat coffee ice cream, laugh at a good joke, hear the rain, or hug me. She would never be there to touch or to be touched. I'd never again hear the sound of her voice, find her opened books, cups of unfinished tea with the used tea bags in them, or smell the odor of her skin after a bath. Empty inside, I became mad at her, and at Dad, and at myself for not being there to listen. Something that should be so easy to do for people who love each other. Why was it so hard?

When would the nagging ache go away? When would I wake up without missing Mom, without my first thoughts in the morning being only of her? I hated each new day. Is this the way Mom lived her life?

Aunt Ellen found the suicide note on my mother's night table next to an open magazine. She didn't show it to me right away. Dad didn't want me to see it at all. I overheard Aunt Ellen say to him, "She isn't a child any more. It's for Beth from her mother. Her last thoughts. Concerns. It's good for Beth to know that they were about her and for her."

"I think some things should be hidden from children. And if Marion was so concerned, tell me why did she do this?"

"Children, yes, depending on the child. Young adults, no. Hiding things doesn't alleviate anything," Aunt Ellen said, exasperated. "Beth can handle it."

"Hasn't she had enough?"

"Yes, she has. Somehow, I hope this will help to put things at rest."

She came upstairs later, peeked past the door, handing me a slip of paper. Mom's stationery, her present to herself last Christmas. "It will be okay, Beth. With time, everything will be okay. I promise." Who was she trying to convince? I turned on the lamp. I had been lying in the dark. The note didn't make me feel that her death was final. Was a suicide note to explain, or to lay on one last guilt trip?

My dearest Beth, I love you. I'll miss you. I hope you'll understand someday. It is difficult being a mother. It's hard just being a human being. Living and existing. I'll always love you. Please don't ever blame yourself.
Mom.

I tucked it in her favorite book, *Silences* by Tillie Olsen, and set the book aside. What was I supposed to understand someday?

twelve

"Did you have a nice time last night?" asked Dad.

"Very nice." I smiled to myself, thinking about it.

"You forgot to leave the telephone number," said Linda.

"Sorry. I'll try to remember next time."

"Linda's not trying to be nosy, we just want to know where you are. We do care," said my father, halfway out the door.

"Dad?"

"Yes, Beth?"

"I know you're going on a business trip for a few nights, so I wanted to let you know I'm going into the city this weekend to play music and not to worry."

"Absolutely not."

"Oh, Dad. Nance is meeting me. Her mother said yes. And I haven't seen her in so long."

I'd better call Nance and invite her when I get home from school. I did miss her, and if she met me, I wouldn't feel as if I was telling a lie.

"Talk to Linda. I've got to run or I'll miss my train. We can discuss it later tonight. Bye, family." He kissed Lisa on the top of her head. "She looks like a little princess."

Lisa was sitting in her pink stretch suit in the middle of the kitchen floor with dribble down her chin and her breakfast pasted on her bib, sucking a rubberized yellow pretzel. I wondered what kingdom she was a princess from.

"Beth, your father and I feel the same on most things. You already know that."

My mother and father often felt oppositely. What did Linda and Dad have that was more special? Whatever it was, I wasn't about to ask her whether or not I could go.

"I thought with your father away these next few days, maybe you could help me out a little around the house and with Lisa? I have a free-lance copy-editing assignment. I haven't done any work since Lisa was born and I want to get back into it again."

I had overheard her on the phone with some editor, saying that she'd have the galleys in by Monday. That wasn't my problem. The only galley I knew was on a ship.

"It's very important to me. I want this publishing house to know I can do both—work and raise Lisa—so they will give me more work."

"I have a life, too," I said.

"I know that. I don't ask so much of you."

"Jonathan's sisters baby-sit. Kerin's twelve, and Rachel's fourteen."

"Thanks. But no thanks." She slammed the dishes in the sink. "I'll look over the galley proofs when everyone goes to sleep."

I decided that I wasn't going to feel guilty. Why should I help her? Who helped my mother? Tough. I was nice enough to tell them I was going into the city. I told Dad, really; he's the one who brought Linda into the act. I was going on Saturday whether they liked it or not.

"You like to ruin things," said Linda.

"What?"

"I know you've had it rough and you're entitled to fun. I was a teenager once, too. And you more than anyone else should be enjoying yourself after what your mother put you through."

"How dare you say my mother did something to me! It's my father's and your fault. She was left all alone."

"My fault?" Linda looked incredulous.

"You made it so my father would never return. Especially by having a baby."

"I think you're a bit confused."

"I've never been clearer. Don't tell me how I am. Who are you to boss me around?"

"I'm not telling you what to do. I'm trying to guide you through a difficult period. I am your stepmother."

"Don't you ever use that word. You could never be a mother to me. You're so uptight. You're such a . . ."

"Such a what?"

"Forget it. I can hardly wait until I graduate next year."

"That makes two of us." Linda bit her lip.

I picked up my books and left. I was so angry, I didn't close the door. I saw her crying. She wiped her eyes with a dish towel as she stood over the kitchen sink. Her head jerked up, she caught me watching her. Our eyes met. Hers were red and swollen. What did she matter? In September, my senior year would begin. Then graduation. I'd be free to do as I wanted. Not here. I was afraid this next year would seem like forever.

During morning classes, my body was there, but my mind was elsewhere. Madame Glass called on me, but I asked to be excused. In the bathroom at the end of the dimly lit hall, the toilets smelled from cigarettes and joints; the stale air made me feel weary. I opened the window, praying I wouldn't throw up, and rested the palms of my hands on the filthy sill for support, breathing in the fresh air deeply. The warm breeze brushed across my cheeks, refreshing me like a soft washcloth. It was beach weather. Soon it would be June. Malted milk shakes, sticky car seats on long afternoon outings, and fireflies. Mom and I would probably have gone to the Cape again and rented the same bungalow on the water for two weeks from Mrs. McIvers. She was a widow earning her living from people like us who came out every summer. When I came home from the last day of school each year, Mom always helped me to arrange neat bundles, in preparation, on my bed and bureau: T-shirts, bikinis, towels, tiny-flowered or paisley-printed dresses with spaghetti straps, cutoff jeans, jogging shorts, my white drawstring pants, thongs, and a plastic bag for my toothbrush, musk oil, perfumes, makeup, nail clippers, and emery boards. Instead, this July I would probably have to take trigonometry over again, because I had failed most of the exams. Baskin-Robbins needed someone to work part-time on the afternoon shift. I'd see if I could do both. The only thing I was going home to today, and it still didn't feel like home, was Linda's eyes piercing through me.

I heard shuffling and voices in the hall. I left the bathroom as classes were changing and Jonathan passed by.

"What's wrong?"

"I don't feel so hot."

"Maybe you're getting sick again?"

"I don't think it's physical."

"What's the matter?" He put his arm on my shoulder.

I didn't answer.

"Let me see your program."

I fished in my bag and gave him my crumpled schedule.

"We have study hall the same time today. I'll meet you at one and we'll split after lunch."

"You mean cut classes?"

"I only have Spanish left."

"I have health ed. after study hall."

"You can skip that."

"I guess so. It's not like it's my trig class."

"Right. So you'll fail jumping."

"I've never cut a class before. Won't they catch us?"

"We'll go out the side door in the back near the lunchroom where they collect the garbage. I've got orchestra practice. See you after that."

I met Jonathan at lunch. He was with his two friends Peter and Kevin from our music class. They stopped as I approached. Peter's eyes darted toward Kevin's.

"What's the big secret?" I smiled mischievously.

"We were kidding about places in town where you can go to be alone," said Jonathan.

"When you don't own a car or a van," added Kevin.

"Oh," I said. "I don't know this town well enough."

"You will," said Peter, nudging Jonathan.

"I can think of one place," said Peter. "Near Lighthouse Road on the beach. I ride my bike there."

"We thought of that already," said Kevin. "How 'bout the cemetery next to the Montessori School?"

"That eighteenth-century weed patch?" asked Jonathan. "There are beer cans all over the headstones."

"The field near the Elementary School? The sand pits?"

"Too many flies. It's like a swamp there, Kevin," said Peter, laughing.

"The hill up from Walton Junior High?"

"This guy's got a school fetish," retorted Peter. "Are you hung up on a teacher? Ms. Rose?"

"Yuck," said Kevin. "Then you name a better place."

"The Duck Pond near Jonathan's. Cross over the brook on the wooden bridge and keep walking up the path. It gets very thick back there from the overgrown leaves and tangled roots. No one can see from the road if you go behind the bushes."

"Everyone goes there." Kevin beamed. "Didn't you know that?"

"I never saw you there." Peter smirked.

"I never saw you, either," said Kevin, "but who's looking? Anyway, it's like Roosevelt Raceway. People are lined up like parking spaces."

"You two are really cool," said Jonathan.

"Don't you know anywhere indoors?" It was the first time I had said anything. Three pairs of eyes turned in my direction.

Peter scratched his curly black hair. "Larry Klugue trespasses on boats anchored at the marina."

"That isn't right," I said.

"There's always those deserted greenhouses on old Mr. Hatton's farm. He's some guy with ten acres who sells organic vegetables," continued Kevin. "He doesn't use any sprays, all natural produce. Only, he uses a gun if he catches you on his property."

"He's harmless," said Jonathan.

"My parents' basement was always a place to go," said Kevin, "but I didn't have anyone to bring there until this year. Now that I do, my father's got it into his head to turn it into a family room. Sheetrock, exposed beams, and electrical wiring are everywhere. I'm afraid I'll get crucified on a nail protruding from a stud or shocked with enough voltage to become Frankenstein's understudy. And then what would I do for dates?"

"Go out with tall women," said Jonathan.

"Cute," said Kevin sarcastically.

"I have a place to be alone," said Jonathan.

"Where?" Kevin and Peter were like two dogs waiting for steak bones.

"My father's dry-cleaning store. He has a large padded ironing-pressing board the width of a king-sized bed. And I have a key."

"You lucked out," grimaced Peter.

I looked at Jonathan. How many girls had been with him in that store? Would he ever take me there? Would I go? Or want to? I had never been alone with someone in the way they were talking about. How would I know when I was ready?

We left after lunch and took the bus as far as it could go down by the beach, walking the rest of the way. I dug my feet into the sand, watched the sun on the water, and talked to Jonathan about nothing special, just to talk to him. We lay on a sand dune, making a pillow of straw, driftwood, and his shirt. He touched my forehead, kissed my eyelids, then my neck, and went on top of me. I kissed him back near his sideburn. My hips rose off the ground until we found our own rhythm, as if we were dance partners. What did he look like beneath the bulge of his zipper in those tight Levi's? It was as if a rock was rubbing against my thigh. I lost myself in the waves of our movement as we felt each other's body. I could feel the smile on my face. He began to unzip my jeans, but I moved his hand away. He rolled on his back, closing his eyes. I watched the wind blow through his hair.

"Are you mad?" I whispered.

"Of course not. Are you?"

"No." I ran my finger down the profile of his face.

"You haven't slept with anyone yet," he said.

I didn't need to answer. It wasn't a question. It was obvious.

"You have." I knew the answer already.

He nodded.

"Anyone in school?"

"Yes."

"Do I know her?"

"Come on, Beth. It's unimportant who I've been with, I'm glad I met you."

"I'm happy I met you, too, but I can't help being curious."

"Me, neither. Did you have a boyfriend at home?"

"He wasn't really my boyfriend."

"Aha. You have a past also."

"Some past."

And we both laughed.

We followed the outline of the shore, throwing pebbles in the Sound. I still didn't have any answers. All I felt was that *if* I slept with someone while I was still in high school, before I was engaged, married, or maybe living with a guy, I trusted him. In my life right now, there were only two people I trusted, Aunt Ellen and Jonathan.

thirteen

When I got back, I could feel Linda's eyes surveying me.

"Your father's working late tonight. He's leaving very early in the morning for Houston, so you might not see him. He told me to talk to you about going into the city. You know how he feels, and how I feel. I know you'll do what you want, I can't sit on you, but be careful, Beth. You're looking for trouble."

"What kind of trouble am I looking for in the middle of Manhattan in broad daylight with millions of people around me?"

"That's not the kind I'm talking about."

"Then what kind?"

"Your attitude."

"What's my attitude?"

"Hostile. I've never done anything to harm you. It's hard on me, too."

I stomped upstairs to study my trigonometry notes. First, I went into the bathroom to rinse the sand off between my toes. Stretched out on the bathmat, I did twelve sit-ups, twenty leg stretches, ten on each leg, and forty jumping jacks to make up for cutting gym. Or was it to let off steam about Linda?

Tossing my books on the bed, I rested on my side, trying to concentrate on my trigonometry textbook. I vowed to do everything in my power to avoid taking math again. A scratching at the skylight distracted me. A black crow was pecking at the plastic bubble. Rotating the rod, I opened the skylight, shooing the bird away through the screen. It was beginning to get dark; the cooling air rushed down the skylight past my open window. There was a gentle knock at my door.

"Can I come in? It's me, Linda."

I got out of bed again to let her in.

"Do you want to go for pizza in the shopping center with me and Lisa?"

"They make crummy pizza there."

"We could drive to Angelo's."

"Couldn't you bring me back a slice? I have a trig quiz tomorrow to study for. I really shouldn't come." Was this me, making excuses to pass up pizza for trigonometry?

"It won't be too long. Lisa gets cranky sitting

in one spot. I thought it would be nice. Just the three of us."

"Okay. I'll get my jacket."

The five-minute drive to Angelo's seemed long. It would have been easier to forgive this morning's and afternoon's angry words if we were mother and daughter, but we weren't.

I held Lisa as Linda locked up the car. She yanked at my silver hoop earring and sucked a strand of my hair. As I carried her into the pizza parlor, she felt like a panda in my arms. Linda tucked her securely into a booster seat at the table and then went to the ladies' room. One hand on her tiny birdlike shoulder, the other on her chest, I supported her so she wouldn't slip. She seemed so fragile it frightened me, and I started getting a headache. Luckily, Linda came right back.

"Everything okay? Did you order yet?"

"No. Not yet. Could we switch seats?"

"Sure. Not used to infants?"

"I have no reason to be."

"That could easily be remedied." She raised her hand in protest before I said anything. "I'm not starting. Let's have a truce for tonight. Truce?"

"Truce," I said.

Linda ordered a beer.

"You drink beer?"

"Sometimes even out of the bottle."

This time she poured it into a wax-paper cup.

"I always figured you to be a white-wine person. That's what you drink with Dad."

"Sometimes I like beer, too."

We talked about school, Lisa, publishing, and the summer. Never about Dad. Never about Jonathan. I felt lighter when we drove home. Surprisingly, my headache disappeared. Lisa gurgled in her car seat the whole way back. I turned around. She looked like my father. Why hadn't I noticed it before?

When we got home, Linda said, "I had a good time."

"I've got to study now."

"I hope you did, too. Angelo makes the best pizza," said Linda. "I'll tell your father goodbye for you when he gets home. Anything else?"

"No," I said. "Good night."

I started up the steps and paused. "Linda . . ."

"Yes?"

"Angelo does make the best pizza in town."

"I'm glad you enjoyed it and decided to come. Sleep tight."

In my mind, I completed the line . . . "and don't let the bedbugs bite." Mom used to say that every night.

fourteen

I stacked sheet music in a canvas bag before I went to bed, because I planned on leaving early Saturday morning. But I overslept. I tried to sneak out past Linda.

"Beth? Is that you?"

Should I run out the door without answering?

"Jonathan called. He said that he couldn't wait any longer or else he'd miss his flute lesson."

So I'd be going into the city alone.

"Don't be home late."

She knew. And she wasn't going to make a scene. Was she telling me it was okay?

"All right," I shouted back.

I met Nance at the lion statue in front of the Public Library on Fifth Avenue. When she spotted me, she ran down the steps. We hugged and jumped up and down.

"You look terrific!"

"So do you," I said.

"Did you do something to your hair?"

"It's the sun. I've been going to the beach a lot with Jonathan. We're surrounded by sand out on the Island."

"You're still seeing him."

"It's been over two months. I haven't seen you in four! I can't believe it."

"Neither can I. I miss you, Beth. It hasn't been the same on the block since you left. My mom said it's getting too expensive to call from Westchester to Long Island."

"I haven't made any friends. Not like you."

"I've applied for early admission to Sarah Lawrence."

"That's great, Nance. My mother's alma mater."

"Gee, Beth, I'm sorry, I forgot."

"That's okay. I haven't even thought about college. Don't you want to go out of town?" I asked.

"It's not bad at home. Eventually, I could save money working and get my own apartment, or a place on campus."

"All I think about is when I graduate."

"To do what?" asked Nance.

"Just to be free. From them," I said.

We put our arms around each other's waist and waited for the M1 bus that would take us down to

Soho. Nance gave me the gallery tour. Her art teacher, whom she had a crush on, had sculpture on exhibit in a loft on West Broadway. We looked up at a thirty-foot ceiling and watched the longest tie-dyed scarf I'd ever seen swirl in the breeze of a fan. A little plaque the size of an index card said, "1969 Soft Sculpture No. 93 On Loan from the Estate of Dr. and Mrs. Seymour Lipschitz."

"He was ahead of his time," said a bearded man next to a punk-looking person. "Everyone was into color field then."

"Is that a male or female?" I whispered.

"I don't know." Nance giggled. "Did you see those leather pants?"

"What do you think of the show?" I asked.

"All I can think of is a word my grandmother used. *Shmatteh.* She could have done a lot of kitchen floors with that work of art."

"What's that? It sounds weird."

"A rag."

"I'm bored. Let's go to Secondhand Millie's."

Some of the clothes were romantic. Most of it was junk. I bought some old postcards from Paris that people sent to one another during World War II. Nance dragged me into an antiquarian bookstore with classical baroque music playing and green glass lamps that were hung so low they almost touched our heads. We strolled to Chinatown, ate sweet pork buns, looked through sleazy fabrics lined up like gigantic Tootsie Rolls on long, flimsy aluminum tables, and then we took the uptown train to meet Jonathan and his friends.

"Jonathan, this is my best friend, Nance, the girl-friend I told you about."

He squeezed my shoulder. I felt good about that. Nance noticed. He introduced her to the rest of the band.

"Does the band have a name?" she asked.

"No. We're just here to make some money," said Yvonne. "With Beth's music, maybe we'll cut a single and then have to think of a name."

I said, "Jumping the gun a little, aren't you?"

"Hand it over. We'll see if I'm off base." Yvonne studied the music. "Let's play," she said to the band.

"The Purple Pedigrees. How's that? Since you all go to Juilliard. Classy?" asked Nance.

"More like the Mangy Mongrels," said Yvonne, laughing, "with this bunch."

The band sight-read my music. It sounded awful to me. I couldn't bear to watch and wait as they played the same piece over and over.

"Come for a walk." I nudged Nance as she was bobbing her head in beat to the drum and making eyes at Max playing lead guitar. "I can't take this."

"No. It's great. I want to stay. It's *your* music."

"I'll be back soon."

"I'll be here." She whispered, "Jonathan's a real hunk."

I laughed. I knew Nance in my bones. I hoped we'd always be close, even though she lived so far away. Poking around in stores and staring in shop windows as though I was really interested in the merchandise killed some time. Who was I kidding? I was dying inside. At a corner newsstand, I bought a magazine and found a bench to sit down on. I must have read the same page for ten minutes, until I decided to go back and own up to my fate. There weren't as many people listening as I hoped for. Failure was awful. I remained at a distance until more passersby filled up the empty space near the band. Slowly, I came closer, immersing myself in the crowd that was forming, so no one would know I was the composer. Watching them watch, swaying when they swayed, acting as if I was one of them wasn't easy. When a few pieces were over, everyone applauded; some threw money in the open guitar case. Should I clap at my own music? Pretend? I threw in a nickel, so if anyone was looking, they wouldn't catch on.

"You're worth at least a dime. Maybe a whole quarter," said Jonathan as he leaned over.

"Leave me alone."

"Once we got it right, they loved it. Why can't you accept success? It's too much to feel good?" He made a funny face.

I couldn't keep from laughing, though I tried.

"Your stuff is good," said Yvonne.

"Great sound," added Max.

"We're packing up in an hour to get a bite and hear a concert in the park. Do you want to come?" asked Yvonne.

"Will it be on very late?" I asked.

"Come on. It's a free Elton John concert in the Sheep Meadow," coaxed Max.

"I've got to call my mom," said Nance. "I can't pass that up."

When Nance's mother said yes, I figured it would be okay if I went, too, but I was afraid that if I called Linda she'd say no. We all chipped in and bought the fixings for a picnic. Sprawled out next to Jonathan, I rested my head on his chest, listening to his heart beat. Closing my eyes, I soaked in the peacefulness. Should I call Linda? Let her know where I am? It was too late. The concert was going to begin. Some warm-up band was playing to the audience to psych us up. No one was listening, but everyone was in the mood. It was free. You could get high just breathing. Jonathan was saying something to me, but the music was so loud all I saw were his lips mouthing, "You're beautiful." Nance was sitting next to Max. Yvonne gyrated alone with the air. The concert ended at around eleven. I kissed and hugged Nance, leaving her and Max at Forty-second Street.

Jonathan whispered in my ear, "We could stop off at my father's store for a little while. The subway's right here that goes into Queens. We'll be there in five minutes, and we can hop on the L.I.R.R. at Woodside going home."

"Won't we get back too late? It's eleven already."

"Beth, if you're nervous, we won't."

"Let's catch the subway," I said.

His father's store had fluorescent orange signs plastered over the front window. Same Day Service. Shirts Cleaned Two for One. Sale Lasts This Week Only. Pants Hemmed While-U-Wait. Summer Fur

Storage. With the letters COLD zigzagged like an ad for Eskimo pies. Inside, there was a glass chandelier over the cash register. Crystal beads clinked in the silence. Heavy brass letters glowed behind the front counter. Fine dry cleaning. Tailoring. Since 1906. Since 1906? Clear plastic bags of pants, dresses, skirts, three-piece double-breasted suits hung like corpses of meat on the metal racks.

"Nice," I lied. I didn't want to hurt him.

"My mom calls this place Flatbush Renaissance. Dad says the customers like it decorated this way."

I looked down at the burned holes from cigarette butts in the worn turquoise carpeting, pushing my sandal over one hole to hide it. There were fliers on the counter that said: "Ask About Our Custom-Made Suits. Fit Your Body like a Glove."

Lights filtered in from passing cars, flashing neon signs in an all-night record store and takeout deli, and from apartments. Who were those people with lights burning in their one room, curtains opened, shades up, with nothing to hide or protect? I stared up above and saw salmon-pink and nauseous hospital-green walls. Mom and I painted everything bright, clean white or antique eggshell. How could these people sleep over a bar or next to an elevated train track? Maybe they became deaf after a while? Or numb to the way they lived? A girl my own age and a young child leaned out the window, watching a dog bark at a man resting against a fire hydrant. How did she do her homework? Was it her child? Had she dropped out of school, and was she living on welfare? An older woman beckoned them in, pulling the tattered venetian blind down.

Jonathan fumbled for the light switch. "Over here." He led me blindly to the back of the store. "I can't seem to get these lights on. It's strange. There's always a small one that's left on to prevent robberies."

"A likely story," I joked, "and when you get a car I bet you'll run out of gas."

"Comedian."

"My eyes are adjusting. I can see you clearly now," I said.

"What were you staring at before?" asked Jonathan as he smoothed down a blanket for us to sit on.

"Oh, nothing. Just people."

"Which people?"

"Out there." I pointed to the front of the store. "I feel sorry for myself and all I have to do is look outside, or listen to the news, and there's always something worse and more horrible than I could ever imagine. Then I feel guilty for feeling bad about myself and my problems. But it doesn't help them go away. Do you ever feel that way? Or am I crazy?"

"Sure I do. Everyone does."

"What bothers you?"

"I think about more immediate things. Like, will I have enough money for music books, lessons, albums, tapes, my commute into the city, a Rampal concert. How can I shut up my sisters and brothers so I can study? When are my parents going to stop bugging me about my hair and my room? I don't try to solve world crises. I also don't have your kind of heady problems to deal with. My biggest concern is getting a music scholarship at a good college, maybe Juilliard."

"Do you believe in fate? That there's a master plan deciding it all?"

"I have faith in my music. It's in my power to do good or bad."

"What about the people who try so hard and get nowhere? Like some of the ones in the apartments up there?"

"You need talent, luck, and elbow grease. I've been busting my chops for my music for I don't know how long."

"Maybe a guardian angel will help you?"

"Ha."

"What about God?" I asked.

"What about him?"

"Her. Do you believe in God?"

"If there is one, I hope that he, she, or it is listening and gets me into Juilliard."

"God, get Jonathan into Juilliard!" I screamed.

Jonathan laughed and looked surprised at my change of mood. His cheek rubbed roughly against my own. In his mouth, I tasted the sangría we shared earlier during the concert, once again. He moved his hand under my peasant blouse, untying the thin tassels of colored embroidery thread down the front, kissing my breasts. I felt his hand traveling downward. Was it too soon? Should I? I smiled, thinking about our first day. We had already shared many secrets and I felt as if I had always known him. There are just some people you feel that way about. He had seen me physically sick and emotionally vulnerable about my mother, and had been there for me. Wanting to be near him, I no longer thought, I reacted. And as if I willed it, he did exactly what I dreamed of, in the way I wanted him to. I hoped I was doing the same for him. Now that I had a gentle, loving person like Jonathan, the reality was better than the fantasy. After we soaked in each other's warmth, we rolled away from one another to regain our breath and consciousness, to return from some dream. The air chilled the evaporating beads of sweat on my skin as I began slipping on my blouse. Jonathan cast it aside and pulled me toward him. I nestled my head in his chest and felt it was the safest place in the world to be.

"Shit!" yelled Jonathan, jolting me out of sleep.

"What's wrong?"

"We missed the train. The next one isn't until 1:20!"

"What are we going to do?" I was scared. "Linda's going to murder me."

"My parents aren't going to be too thrilled, either."

"Should we call?"

"It's kind of late. I'd rather not wake them up."

"Do you really think they're sleeping?"

I opened the door quietly. A low light in the hall silhouetted Linda standing with her hands resting on her hips. Somehow, at this point, I didn't think she was worried about whether or not he had walked me to the front door.

"Where have you been?"

"We were at a free concert in Central Park and lost track of time."

"That's obvious. There are no phones in New York City?"

"We just missed the train."

"Which train? I was ready to call the police. Hospitals. I didn't even have that boy's last name or telephone number to call his parents! Are you crazy?" She almost lunged at me. Was *she* crazy? "How could you do this? With your father away?"

"It wasn't deliberate. And that boy's name is Jonathan Schein. I've told you and Dad. I'm sorry about forgetting to give you the phone number again. You act like I did something to you personally."

"Didn't you?"

"I knew you'd be mad."

"Mad? I'm not mad. I'm livid!"

"I guess I should have called."

"It was more than poor judgment. It's a total lack of consideration. For me, your father, and being a member of this family. I have to be up with Lisa in four hours, as if I could fall asleep now."

"I said I'm sorry."

"Who knew what could have happened? What did happen?"

"I'm a grownup. I can take care of myself."

"You don't know the first thing about being grownup! An adult takes responsibility."

118

Her screaming woke up Lisa.

"Ter-ri-fic!" bellowed Linda. "I'm calling your father first thing in the morning. I don't need to deal with this. Let him. You're his daughter."

"You finally said it."

"You are, aren't you? What's there to admit?" she shouted sarcastically as she backed up the stairs. "I've had it. Up to here." She acted as if she was slicing her neck. In one last outburst, she leaned over the banister: "Why should I worry about someone who doesn't care about me?" I felt smug. Linda had proved she was the bitch I always thought she was. I stayed downstairs until she went into Lisa's room.

When it was quiet, I went upstairs and crawled into bed. The light from Dad and Linda's bedroom filtered under my door. I pulled the covers over my head, trying to concentrate on Jonathan to blot out her presence.

fifteen

When I woke up, I wasn't sure if it was morning or afternoon. I listened for any sounds of Linda or Lisa. Quietly getting dressed, I went down the back stairs to the kitchen, hoping the coast was clear. A note was attached with little daisy magnets to the refrigerator.

Took Lisa to the park. Won't be back for lunch. Jonathan called at eleven. No message. If you plan on going out, be back no later than six, dinner time.

There was no *Dear Beth, Beth,* whatever, at the top of the note, or signature from Linda, which was not like her. She must really be angry and avoiding me as much as I wanted to avoid her. Luckily, she had left for the day. I poured some orange juice to get rid of an awful taste in my mouth, and dialed Jonathan.

He answered, "Hello."

"It's me. Well?"

"My parents were asleep, but they knew."

"How?"

"Parents know everything. They were pissed off I didn't call."

"So was Linda. She was standing at the door like a general."

"You're kidding! My parents said I was inconsiderate, bringing you home at such an hour."

"That's not true."

"Can I see you?"

"Linda will probably be back around four or five, she'd blow her top."

"Just for a little. I miss you."

"Okay, but come here. We'll hang out in the backyard, but you've got to leave before she gets back. Let's play it safe. I'm not in the mood for any confrontations."

"Me, neither. See you soon. I'll ride my bike over."

When Jonathan came over, we started fooling around in my room, but every time I heard a creak in the house, or noise outside, I was afraid it was Linda coming home early, so we stopped.

"This is not playing it safe," I said.

"Far from it. Let's go for a bike ride," said Jonathan.

"Maybe I should stay here, in case Linda comes back?"

"Calm down," he said, walking into the hall. "We won't go far."

"Just in the neighborhood."

In the hot, humid air, we created a slight wind for ourselves. Jonathan pedaled with all his strength. It was difficult keeping up with him, but I tried. Some four- or five-year-olds raced us on their Spiderman Hot Wheels and Chips cycles. Jonathan knew all that stuff from his brother David. We let them win and left grinning faces near the sidewalk. I smelled barbecues, cut grass, and trees as we circled the same streets.

"Is it time for me to head back?"

"Think so." He frowned.

We parked our bicycles a few blocks from the house to say goodbye. I put my hands on his cheeks.

"I'll call you tonight?" he asked.

"Let me call you, instead." And I rode away, looking back for a moment, missing him already.

Linda was still gone when I returned. I made myself a tuna sandwich and called Nance, but no one was home. Sunday was a family day, they probably all went somewhere. My father telephoned and I pretended nothing had happened. Linda obviously hadn't talked to him yet. Was she waiting for him to call so his firm would pay for it? He said he'd be home on Tuesday if the negotiations went the way he planned, and would try Linda later tonight. She walked in shortly after I hung up.

"My father called. He'll try you later."

"Salad and tunafish for dinner."

"I already ate some. Thanks, anyway."

Linda turned away, lifting Lisa out of the stroller that was just inside the kitchen door.

"I'll be upstairs doing my homework."

"Suit yourself."

At around seven-thirty the phone rang. It must be Dad. Linda didn't yell for me to pick it up. I listened for her footsteps. Finally she came up, but went into Lisa's room, and then to the bathroom to bathe Lisa. That's when I slipped downstairs to the kitchen.

"Jonathan, it's me, Beth. I've been in my room over three hours, like a prisoner. I hate it here."

"Can you come over?" asked Jonathan.

"No, I can't. I have to hang up, she's coming."

Rushing over to the cupboard, I pulled out a glass, a bag of pretzels, and then poured some milk and started to my room.

"Don't eat up there, you'll make crumbs."

Putting my glass back on the counter, I gave her a cold stare. Long, narrow sheets of paper with type all over them were spread out on the table near a huge dictionary, a thesaurus, and other thick books. Those must be the galleys she was copy-editing. Linda didn't look up when I went into Dad's den, now her sewing room, to turn on the television. She had taken over that, too. A tiny pattern was stretched tautly on Dad's green felt desk blotter with a dotted-swiss fabric and pins stuck into it like a voodoo doll.

"Turn it down! I can hear it all the way in here," she screamed.

I used the ear plugs so I wouldn't hear Linda's voice complaining one more time.

sixteen

I brushed past Linda with my overstuffed canvas
bag.

"Where are you going so early on a Monday
morning?" asked Linda.

"None of your business."

"That's no way to talk to me."

"Why don't you call Bob?"

I slammed the front door. Should I tell Jonathan? Maybe he'll try to telephone me if I don't show
up in theory? Go to Nance's? Her mother would ask
too many questions. I had only seven dollars on me,
not enough money for both trains. Where should I
go? Where I knew I belonged, and there wouldn't
have to be any explanations, or words.

"What a pleasant surprise!" said Aunt Ellen as she opened the door of her apartment. "Are you off from school today?"

"Oh, Aunt Ellen."

"What's wrong, honey?"

"Everything."

"Sit down."

"Can I have something to drink?"

She came out of the kitchen with a glass of orange juice and her morning coffee. "Talk to me."

"I can't take it, Aunt Ellen."

"Take what?"

"Living there."

"Why?"

"I feel like I'm in prison. They don't understand me. Or Mom. Or even you."

"Me?"

"Dad makes fun of your being a therapist. They're both like robots. Or stiffs."

"What a picture you're painting. Go slower. You've been there four months. Suddenly they turned on you? Why now?"

"Everyone has a breaking point."

"Let's backtrack. What happened, Beth?"

"No big deal. I stayed out late Saturday night, and had a fight with Linda, and she told Dad on me."

"How late?"

I looked away.

"How late?" she repeated.

"About two-thirty," I muttered.

"What an asinine thing to do!"

"I got involved."

"Involved?"

"You know. With Jonathan."

"Beth. I figured you to be more sensible than that. It sounds to me like a lot more was taking place than a simple date if you strolled in at two-thirty in the morning."

"Can't pull anything over on you, Ms. Doctor."

"We'll talk about that later. What did you expect at that hour?"

"That she'd be asleep."

"Anyone with half a conscience wouldn't. You're pretty angry at Linda, aren't you?"

"You're damn right I am."

"I understand. I can't help feeling that way myself sometimes."

The telephone rang. I waved my hands. "Don't tell her I'm here."

Aunt Ellen picked up the phone. "She's fine. I know there's school. I'll drive her back later tonight. Goodbye."

She hung up.

"You gave me away."

"I didn't need to add wood to the fire."

"Why are you so smart?"

"Because I spent my life in school?"

"Seriously."

"I've just lived a little more. I'm not so smart."

"Do you know how much I love you?"

"No. Hum a few bars. Go. Wash up. You're all sweaty from the train ride."

After my bath, I walked into the kitchen,

brushing my damp hair onto a fluffy white towel.

"What smells so good?" I asked.

"Pancakes. For you, dear, anything."

A fire engine charged down Broadway, its siren wailing as if to announce the arrival of summer. Aunt Ellen turned on the air conditioner. We plopped down on the couch, head to toe; I tickled her bare feet.

"Enough!" she screamed, holding her stomach. "Time out." We rested. She had a devilish look in her eye.

"You'd better not," I said. "You said 'Time out,' didn't you?"

"I swear I won't"—as she feigned an attack on my waist and armpits. "I hope you were careful, Beth."

"We were."

"Do you want the name of my gynecologist?"

"Why not?"

Would Mom have been so matter-of-fact? Casual? Was it their seven-year difference in age? Aunt Ellen always seemed somewhere between an aunt and an older sister.

"Did you love the first person you went to bed with?"

"Yes. He was very special."

"Do you still know him?"

"No. I don't."

"I'm scared about being left. Again."

"That makes a lot of sense. Your father left you, in a way. And so did your mother. Don't rush, Beth. You can't create feelings, they have to happen, emerge on their own."

"You think I rushed to hold on to Jonathan? I'm not sorry I did."

"There's nothing to feel guilty about." She put her arms around my neck. "Listen, babe, you've taken a big step. Making love doesn't make you love someone and doesn't make you grownup. Remember how excited you were when you first met Jonathan in April? How you went on about how warm inside, and good, he made you feel? Just talking to him? He touched your mind, too."

"Loving him was like playing my music. I came closer to myself than I've ever been."

Aunt Ellen sighed. "Youth."

"Do you think I'm too young?"

"What's young? You'd probably be in a convent if your father knew. If something seems sincere, then maybe it is right. I can't creep into your heart. I know I feel more at thirty-one than I did at sixteen. My emotions are deeper. I've experienced more."

"Practice makes perfect."

"You're a real joker. I'm not going to preach, judge, or make decisions for you, but I will help if you want me to. I think you know by now what's right for you and what isn't. It's getting late. I have to be at the clinic by ten. You can relax here today."

"Aunt Ellen, one question before you go. And this is a biggie. Is sex different from love?"

"Ugh. Did you have to? I'm still asking that one."

"I let a boy touch me once and I didn't know him very well. It was awful. Deceitful. I didn't really care about him."

"Then you've answered your own question. Haven't you?"

When I got to Dad's, I asked Aunt Ellen to come in with me. Linda and Lisa were sitting in the kitchen having dessert. Whose home was this? This wasn't my family. They seemed calm and peaceful. Was it because I wasn't there?

"I didn't hear you come in." Linda cleared her throat.

"I used my key. Did you want me to ring the bell? Isn't this my *home*, too?"

"Of course it is. Don't be silly. Would you like some coffee, Ellen?" Linda asked politely. Etiquette before anger.

"That would be nice. The Expressway might be jammed going home. There was an accident near the Queens Boulevard exit."

"Was it bumper-to-bumper?"

"It was, going into Manhattan."

Small talk. Traffic. And Ellen was going along with it.

"Beth, could I please speak to Linda?"

"I have to finish up some homework, anyway."

She kissed me and whispered in my ear, "Maybe you could take Lisa upstairs with you so I can talk to Linda without any distractions? I'll call you tomorrow."

"Could I take Lisa up to her room?"

Linda looked shocked, and nervous. "Be careful."

"I will," I said impatiently.

"I'll be up after I finish here."

Lisa felt like a sack of potatoes as she nodded off to sleep.

"More coffee?" asked Linda as I stepped into the hall.

"Half a cup. Fine," said Ellen.

"What's with Beth?"

I paused on the steps.

"You tell me, she lives with you."

"But she *talks* to you," Linda interrupted. "I know I'm not related, but I'm with her the most. Did you see the way she talked to me tonight? So abruptly, with such venom in her tone. What goes on between us creates a lot of friction in the house. I get so much of the flak that should have been going the way of Bob and Marion. I took her for pizza while Bob was away, it was pleasant for a change, and then all this happened. I'd like to help Beth, but she makes it so hard. What can I do?"

"Just keep trying. She's been very hurt. For a long time. Even before my sister died."

I went upstairs and placed Lisa in her crib. She yawned like a gerbil and curled into a fetal position. I moved the light flannel blanket, tucking it under her feet, turned the Mickey Mouse night-light on, and tiptoed out, for a moment wishing I was her.

seventeen

Jonathan and I didn't have any classes together on Tuesdays. I stayed after school to rehearse for the graduation recital, which was less than two weeks off. Jonathan was probably practicing at home. It was easier carrying around a flute than a piano.

When I got home and walked in the front door, my father was coming down the staircase, and motioned me to go into the den.

"I'm pretty disappointed in you, Beth. I thought you were more responsible than to pull a stunt like that."

"I didn't pull anything. It was an accident. We missed the train."

"You shouldn't have been taking the 1:20 in the

first place. You should have been home by midnight at the latest. Is that what time your mother let you walk in?"

"What does Mom have to do with this?" I hated him for that.

"We won't allow it in this house. The real point is, you knew how I felt and you completely disregarded me."

"Linda saw me leave. She didn't stop me."

"She was trying to be understanding."

"Nothing I say can make her wrong."

"Linda is not the issue here."

"Yes, she is."

"She is? How?"

"She's so perfect. She doesn't give me any room to breathe. I just wanted to get away for a little while. She's always saying don't do this or that. Giving me a hard time."

"Linda wants what's best for you. She's concerned about your welfare. Like I am. What you did was wrong."

"Linda wants what's best for Linda."

"You're being unfair. And you know it."

"Who's unfair? You messed up everything in my life. Mine and Mom's."

My father looked at me with those steely blue eyes of his and closed up like a clam, as he did when he and Mom had a fight. Then he surprised me and spoke. "You think it's my fault, what happened to your mother? Don't you?"

"I think it's your fault your wife died."

"Beth, Linda's my wife. For four years. The divorce went through five years ago." Dad walked over to me and tried to put his arm around me, but I backed away, almost ducking. "Don't leave," he said. I knew it was difficult for him to do that. He wasn't a demonstrative person.

"Everyone talks about what happened to Mom like she had some rare blood disease, or as if she was in some catastrophe. She wasn't in a car accident. She killed herself. No one can say it. Mom chose to die. Wasn't it a conscious choice, a way out of her problems? And that's what you and Mom *happened* to leave me with."

My father stepped back and faced the bookcase, running his finger along the spines of the encylopedias.

"I'm not as callous as you think I am. Don't you think I know how rough it has been for you, for all of us? You act like I'm from another planet. I feel the strain, too. I loved your mother once."

I slumped down in the oversized leather recliner, listening to it creak as I moved uncomfortably. Now was my big opportunity, if I ever had one, to ask my father what had been chipping away at my thoughts for years. Was I still afraid?

"Why did you and Mom get divorced?"

"That's from left field."

"Aunt Ellen said I should talk about it. Isn't this as good a time as any?" I wasn't brave enough, so I put it at her doorstep.

"Aunt Ellen," he mumbled. "Talk, talk, talk about your feelings. Therapy. Be in touch with yourself, mumbo jumbo."

"It's better than keeping things inside," I said more boldly.

"You keep them in, don't you?"

"I'm not now."

"That's true. You're not now. How do I answer that question? As if it had a simple answer? This is hard for me. I'm not used to analyzing."

"What about your law cases?"

"That's different."

"How?"

"How?" he echoed. "Analyzing myself, then."

I answered for him, shocked at my own strength. "You're not emotionally involved. It's all at a distance. Like you kept us. You can walk out of that courtroom any time, like you walked out of the house."

He looked aghast.

"I really don't know the answer. Couples argue about little annoying things like squeezing the toothpaste tube in the middle and leaving the cap off. Or allowing the soap in the sink to become soggy. Your mother used to leave her long hairs around the ring of the bathtub. It drove me up the wall. And I always forgot to take out the garbage. I still do."

What was he talking about? Toothpaste? Soap? Bathtub rings? Garbage?

"Mom learned to take out the garbage. I can put your mind to rest."

"Then it grows into bigger irritations: sex, money, goals, desires. It goes on and on."

"Your goals, were they different from Mom's?"

"You could say that. Your mother and I had

basically different attitudes to life. She approached things emotionally. I saw them logically. We were young. Very young." He sighed. "I did with my life what made me happy. Your mother couldn't accept that. Maybe she couldn't acknowledge my success for lack of her own?"

I'd heard those words before. In a way, hadn't Jonathan told me I couldn't accept success? But he was saying I was good when I played my music for him the first time at his parents' house, and when his band played it, too. My father was standing here implying my mother was a failure. And the only one here to defend her was me.

"What do you mean, Mom wasn't a success?" I looked at him standing there as if he were no relation to me at all, a stranger. What was success, anyway?

"Come on, Beth. You know exactly what I mean."

"No, I don't!"

"Your mother never pursued her art. Left things unfinished. Never saw them through until the end. Except one."

"Huh?"

"Her suicide."

I couldn't believe I heard that.

"Marion talked a blue streak about how everyone held her back. Did she do anything about it? Did she try? After I offered I don't know how many times to help her work it out? When you got older? Even after I left? It was a nice complaint to hold on to. Wasn't it? Didn't she hold herself back?"

"What do you know? Nothing! You don't know

the first thing about Mom!" I flung myself out of that recliner, stomping out of his den. "Or me!"

"I'm trying. What more do you want?"

"What more do you?" I asked.

"For you to start living here, with *us*."

I didn't have an answer to that one.

eighteen

"Where have you been?" asked Jonathan when he saw me at school. "I thought you'd call back Sunday night after you had to rush off when Linda was coming. I needed to talk to you."

"Sorry. I couldn't call, so much has been happening. It's been a bad scene since I walked in late. Monday morning, I went to my Aunt Ellen's after the fight with Linda. How am I going to get through this next year? You know what I mean? I spend most of my time in school or at home, without you."

"But I think of you when you're away from me."

"I do, too. It would be so easy to depend on you," I said.

"Can't we lean on each other?"

"I guess so. We are friends."

"Friends? Hello, pal." He slapped me on the back.

"Lovers?" I felt the word sticking in my throat.

"Let's be both."

That sounded nice.

Classes were changing. Mr. Wheldon bumped into us, pushing his wire-rimmed glasses up onto his nose. "You both did very well on the final. My two best students." He winked at me. At least I was doing well in music. I could have hugged him for sharing that news. He was like a koala bear, his slightly pudgy stomach hanging over his belt. "See you at the dress rehearsal on Friday. The June recital already!"

"I'll meet you at three near the bike rack in the parking lot. We have to talk. You have your bike?" asked Jonathan.

"Yes. What's this all about?"

"I'm taking you on a mystery ride."

"You like surprises."

"Who doesn't?"

"Me. I like to know where I'm going."

"Symbolic?"

"Perhaps."

"It's somewhere beautiful."

We rode through busy traffic into a quiet tree-lined road. It was wide and dark, shaded by old oak trees. Lanterns dotted long driveways that led to stately porticos, pools, greenhouses, and tennis courts. What kind of people lived in these homes? I loved to see them lit up at night like dollhouses, each one with a different story to tell. We continued on the road, down a steep hill that twisted and turned sharply. I kept my hands on the brakes the whole way as we flew into glaring sunlight. The change almost blinded me. Morning glories clung to white picket fences and hot-pink petunias trailed near sandy patches. Passing a guardless gate, I saw in front of me a majestic mansion set on a point, surrounded by beach and water, French doors open on every side. Tubs of geraniums lined connecting paths. Hanging pots swayed on awnings.

"What is this place? This isn't someone's home?" I lowered my voice nervously.

"It's the County Club. I busboyed here last season."

"Oh," I said, somewhat relieved. "Is it okay for us to be here?"

"It hasn't opened officially yet. This weekend. But I know everyone."

"I've never seen anything like this except in the movies. How did you get a job here?"

"An old friend of my father's. He's a member."

"It must have been great working here."

"Great, huh. The women never go in the pool. Their hairdos. I'll show you. It's this Olympic-sized aquamarine pool. Unused. They tan their hides until they're like leather. Skin-cancer brown. If they weren't taking a tennis lesson or playing backgammon, who do you think had to wait on them hand and foot? Even their kids wouldn't walk thirty feet to get potato chips."

"How awful."

"Boring is the word."

"I can imagine. I once went with my mother to a luncheon for the historical society. They talked about decorating, who was on what diet, and where they got their legs waxed."

"What's that? Like waxed fruit?"

"Hair removal. In unmentionable areas, too."

"You're joshing."

"I'm not."

"Over here, Beth." We parked our bikes on weathered wooden planks. He pointed to a freshly painted cabana with Astroturf in front. Next to it was another shed with straw matting on the deck and plastic-webbed lawn furniture.

"This is hysterical. A hut away from home. Are we allowed to sit here?"

"We're not harming anything."

I eased onto a chaise longue. "Darling, please hand me my drink. I can't reach the two inches."

"Oh, my pet, free for tennis at two?" Jonathan pretended to puff on a pipe.

"Sorry, dearest. Due for a pedicure and massage."

"See you in the Terrace Room at five. Cocktails. Ciao."

I puckered my lips together, making a phony kissing sound. "Actually, it's really nice here. I'm glad you brought me."

I thought of Nance. She would love it here. "Nance would think she's in a time warp. In a Monet painting. Did Max call her?"

"I think so. Maybe we could double?"

"That would be fun."

We made love on the floor of the cabana. I could feel the Astroturf digging into my back. It was like a bed of hair curlers.

I turned around and Jonathan burst out laughing. "You look like my kid brother's Lego and Bristle Blocks sets rolled into one!"

"Thanks a lot."

We put cushions from the chaise longue on the floor. I heard something.

"What's that sound?"

"No one's there. Stop worrying."

He laughed. I rubbed my fingers through the hair on his chest. And we began again.

Later we got dressed and went into the snack bar.

"Jonathan!" A dark, heavyset man with curly jet-black hair and a mustache screamed out.

"Napoli! Beth, this is the best cook on the Island!"

"In America!" Napoli corrected.

"The most modest, too."

"What brings you here?" Napoli slapped him affectionately on the side of his head.

"Showing my girlfriend the sights."

Girlfriend. That sounded good.

"Want the usual?"

"Sure. Why not?"

Napoli went into the back freezer.

"What's he doing?"

"You'll see."

Napoli returned, balancing two frosted glasses. "To my favorite customer and his pretty friend!"

"To chocolate egg creams!" toasted Jonathan.

"To summer!" I smiled, raising my glass as we clinked them together. "And success at our June recital!"

"Enjoy," said Napoli as he went back into the kitchen.

"Beth, I have something to tell you."

"Hmm?" I asked, making obnoxious noises with my straw sucking the last drops of soda. "Yes," I said, straightening my back on the high stool like an attentive student.

"I'm going away to work as a waiter in the Catskills this summer. My Uncle Morty got me the job."

"You're *what*? How long have you known this?"

"Only a week. Sort of. I wasn't positive until Sunday night."

"You found out a week ago and you didn't tell me?"

"Beth, you haven't been the easiest person to reach since Sunday."

"How could you lead me on?"

"Lead you on?"

"Make love, and then leave."

"I don't want to leave you. I'm going away for a little while to make some money. A lot of money in tips, for college. I could come home for a weekend."

"You won't."

"There's the phone. We could write."

"I'm not writing you."

"Don't be like this."

I drew away and slipped off my stool.

"Where are you going? Beth!" He grabbed my arm. "I love you."

I ignored him and ran past the pool to the beach. He ran after me. "Please understand. I wasn't sure I was going until this Sunday. Do you really think I want to leave you? I need the money, in case I don't get a scholarship next fall."

I felt guilty. He was twisting everything. "You should have told me. You were dishonest. Maybe I wouldn't have made love with you if I knew you were leaving?"

"Why?"

"Don't be so thick. I'm not casual, Jonathan. You know that I've never been with anyone like I've been with you. It meant a lot to me."

"To me, too."

"Not enough."

"You're wrong."

"I know I'm not acting very liberated, but I don't care. I slept with you because I trusted you. Trust means a great deal to me and I feel our trust has been broken. I don't know if I will feel the same way again."

"I'm sorry. I really am."

"So am I. I thought you were different."

"You've got it all wrong, Beth. It's not like I want to be away from you."

"I wouldn't have had the time to see you, anyway. I'll probably fail trig and have to go to summer school. And I forgot to tell you, I've got a job at Baskin-Robbins." Tomorrow, first thing after school, I would apply for the position.

Without speaking, we bicycled up the tedious hill. For the first time, I wished I was alone, without Jonathan.

nineteen

It all seemed so pat. Girl meets boy. They fall in love. Boy leaves girl. They fall out of love. The awful part was, I couldn't stop thinking about Jonathan. Anger and all. I saw him at the dress rehearsal, he tried to speak to me, but I felt too hurt.

The June recital was the best assembly program Bleeker had ever had, at least the school newspaper said so. Jonathan slipped a note in my locker, telling me I played beautifully. I wrote a short note back, thanking him, but ripped it up before putting it in his locker. He telephoned several times before he left, but I didn't talk to him. I got the job at Baskin-Robbins, and prayed I'd have the stamina not to gain weight. It was like putting a squirrel in a nut shop.

In my mood, I feared wallowing in the hot-fudge sauce. Summer school began at eight in the morning; I had the bad luck of getting Mr. Hyde for trigonometry again, with his white socks, dandruff, and open fly. This wasn't my year.

Every day I checked the mailbox, torturing myself. Not even a postcard. Then the kid next door came over and handed me a letter dated a week earlier. My address was 7 Lobster Lane and this said 5. Couldn't Jonathan get it right?

I went up to my room, closed the door, and sat on my bed staring at the handwriting I had seen so often in his music notes. Ripping off the corner of the envelope, I slid my finger along the edge. Waiting a moment, I took a deep breath and unfolded the letter. July 4. It was already the eleventh.

Dear Beth,

I'm sorry everything turned out the way it did. I don't consider our relationship ended. I want you to know that when I said I loved you, I meant it. I've never told anyone that. Please forgive me. This letter is short, but I have a big weekend ahead of me here and I have to hit the sack early tonight.

Love,
Jonathan

I put the letter in the back of my dresser drawer, hidden next to my underwear and socks. Pushing my trigonometry assignment aside, I opened my composition pad and started writing a new song. This time, with lyrics. I slept better than I had for a week.

July 12

Jonathan—

I just wanted you to know that my address is 7, not 5, Lobster Lane. I didn't want you to bother our neighbors at number 5. I received your note a week late. I'm busy with work, school, and my music. When I get a chance, I go to the beach. Thought you might like this postcard with the elephant taking a vacation in the country. He's packing his trunk. Get it?

Beth

July 14

Dear Beth,

I got back from lunch and found your postcard. It felt so good to see it lying there on my bed, even though I can see from your tone you're still angry. (No "Dear Jonathan" and just "Beth.") Please don't be. Can I call you? Or will you hang up? I have the afternoon off. I thought I'd swim and sleep. This job is rough, but I have fun, too. This new friend Eddie (he's a musician too, plays the drums) did a crazy joke on this guy who smokes cigars in our faces and tips badly. He hid a golf ball in a scoop of cream cheese during Sunday brunch. I wonder how his bialy tasted. We didn't wait around to find out. Eddie's planning on putting sugar in the salt shaker if he's still here next weekend. Got to go.

Love, Jonathan

July 16

Dear Jonathan,

I wouldn't hang up on a long-distance phone call. That nasty, I'm not. Thanks a lot for your postcard. Real cute. Two hippos in a bathtub eating ice cream. Is that a subtle comment on your expectation of my figure by the end of this summer? Your sister Kerin came in to get a cone the other day and says hi. Your mother wants to know why you don't write.

> Notice the "Dear"
> Beth

P.S. That guy Eddie sounds like a jerk.

July 16

Dear Beth,

   I'm not waiting for an answer. I'm calling you to-morrow night after I get off.

> I miss you. J.

July 17
midnight

Dear Jonathan,

   I hate to admit it, but here goes. I can't sleep. It was great hearing your voice again after all these weeks. I didn't realize how much I miss you, too. Maybe I shouldn't tell you this, but after I hung up I was very depressed. I wanted to be next to you, having you hold me, feeling your skin next to mine. I could be leaving myself open for disappointment again, but that's the chance I'll have to take.

   It's great that you put together a band up there and found enough people on the staff who are into music. Are they good? Are you performing anywhere yet? How many of you? I miss the band now that everyone is away this summer. Yvonne called once. Have to go.

Linda's knocking at my door, probably to ask why I'm up so late.

B.
With Hippo Hugs

July 17 late

Dear Beth,

We've got to see each other soon. It's been too long. I've thought over what we fought about and you were right. I should have told you earlier that I was thinking of going away. I guess I was afraid of losing you and I did know somewhere inside of me how you'd react. I can't help that. I needed the money. In certain ways, my music comes first. That doesn't mean you don't enter into things. You do. Always.

Jonathan

July 20

Dear Jonathan,

I'm writing this on the beach, where I can think, closer to where we've been together. The water is the same cobalt blue. Driftwood is strewn on the dunes. A seaplane just took off over the inlet, and I thought of how we fantasized about jet-setting off somewhere, someday.

I received your letter. We were both wrong, and right. Are we going back into things too quickly? Maybe I am? What do you think?

Love always,
Beth

Dear Jonathan,

Are you O.K.? I haven't heard from you. Did you get my last letter? Are you upset by what I said?

Trigonometry is trying. My new motto. I met a very nice girl in my class who I study with for quizzes. Louise Casalle. Do you know her? She's heard of you, boy genius.

Linda has been saner since she got a mother's helper three mornings a week. Some neighborhood kid, thirteen, in between Kerin's and Rachel's ages, munching on celery and carrot sticks all the time. She folds the wash, does some dishes, but mainly walks Lisa to the playground or the Duck Pond.

Lisa was a year old this week. Time flies. Linda and my father had a big party for Linda's drooling relatives. My dad's parents live in Florida and couldn't fly up. I would have liked them to. I haven't seen them since the funeral. (It's still hard to think about it.) They sent a telegram and a stuffed Snoopy the size of a small child. Lisa wore this pink ruffled dress and white pinafore. Linda's parents bought a sound projector and camera for the occasion. Everyone kept trying to make Lisa do something clever and cute. Poor kid. All she wanted to do was smear the chocolate cake. And she did. I bought her a china Peter Rabbit music box. My father said he was glad I knew how to save my money because many young people didn't. Linda said she was touched. I think she was. Her parents said it might be a collector's item one day, as they turned it upside down to see the manufacturer's name. I just hope Lisa doesn't break it. She already tried to bite off one of the ears.

You mentioned seeing each other soon. Nance's family is going to take a long weekend in a bungalow colony on a lake near your hotel, I think in August when her dad's vacation begins. She and I are trying to figure out how I could go with them. Max, as you know, is a music counselor at a camp, so she could visit him, too. (They've been writing to each other.) I'll let you know if there is any good news.

Write soon. Beth.

P.S. If we go, we're going to talk her parents into stopping off at the farm where my old cat Cindy lives now. It's on the way. The family I gave her to wrote a letter saying she had five kittens. Cindy a mother! I can't believe it. I guess she adjusted to her new life.

P.P.S. Is it cold in the country at night? Do I need long johns?

July 27

Dear Jonathan,

I'm glad you called. Sorry you had a sore throat. Maybe it's from working all day and playing with the band all night? Is the lead singer a waitress at your hotel or does she live up there year-round? I'm looking forward to hearing you perform. Nance's parents said that it's okay with them if it's cleared with mine. That should take some convincing. Do you have a number where I can reach you, or is that too difficult?

Cross your fingers,
Beth

Dear Jonathan,

My father spoke to Nance's parents and agreed to let me go with them. It's the weekend of August 7. We should be up there by Friday evening. They are happy you went away. They felt I was too young to be so involved, that you were a bad influence, "reckless" is how they put it, and that I was ignoring my school-work. Dad said that he was pleased I was doing some-thing constructive this summer. I'm finally passing math. Got an 83 on the last test! Let me know your time-off hours. I've got your bunk / cabin number, etc. I'm sending you a surprise! By express.

> Happy 18th Birthday
> Love and Kisses xxxx
> Beth

Dear Beth,

Great news! You're coming. I can hardly wait to see you. It's been so long. Thanks for that CARE pack-age filled with goodies. You're crazy, but I needed it. Especially the razor blades. The canteen gets low and when I get into town it's too late. I loved the old Edith Piaf record. The Meatloaf T-shirt fits just right. Will the glitter come off in the laundry? Fifty Hit Tunes from Those Fabulous Fifties came in handy for our gig at this sleazy bar named Joe's. Was the jockstrap a joke? Or a hint? Don't worry, I'm not hanging out all over Ellen-ville. I've been reading the Woody Allen paperback when I get a chance. (Free time, what's that?) He's a riot. I hope you don't mind me sharing the blondies. Were those just walnuts I was biting? Ha. Ha. I've never heard of blondies. They tasted as if you mated a chocolate-chip cookie and a brownie. Eddie is hooked. So am I. Please bring up more when you come. (I'll pay you back.)

Love,
Jonathan

P.S. Maybe you should burn these letters after you read them? That's all we need—for Linda and your dad to find them, if they don't already know.

August 5

Dear Jonathan,

Two more days! I'm all packed. To answer your question, I'm not getting rid of your letters. I hide them in with my underwear.

I'm getting used to Linda and living in Bayview. She's freelancing for those publishers, and leaves me alone more. I guess she's too busy, or more relaxed now that she has a baby-sitter—though Linda will never be laid back.

Louise and I have become closer. She's pretty good in trig, considering we're all flunkies. I'm doing in the low eighties. Not bad, huh? Louise has the same coloring as you. Blond hair, blue eyes, and a sprinkling of freckles. Mentally, her head is in a different place. No great aspirations. Which is what I need. A friendship on the light side. She wants to be an airline stewardess. I told her it's like being a floating waitress, but she insists it's très glamorous. I've also made friends with a girl who is on my shift at Baskin-Robbins. A perfect match for Eddie. Her name is Robin Brodsky. She was in your homeroom. During our slow periods, she concocts gross sundaes: peanut-butter-and-jelly ice cream (the special this month) with maple-walnut sauce, raspberry syrup, bananas, and whipped cream. No cherry; it has red dye. And get this. A pimento instead!

I feel better about everything. With two new friends, next term should be okay. Last term wasn't so bad. I met you, didn't I?

There's something I've been meaning to tell you. I knew you before I knew you, which means I saw you mowing the lawn across the street from my dad's house the first Saturday morning in April. (How come you weren't at a flute lesson? I wondered about that when we first spoke on the train and you were going to Juilliard.) I wanted to meet you. To know you. I thought you were gorgeous. It rained. You disappeared. I thought I'd never see you again. Little did I know I would be telling you this months down the road. A lot has happened since that morning. I've changed. Even the word "hunk," which I used to describe you before I knew your name, seems immature. It feels good and sad at the same time. I just wanted you to know this. See you soon.

All my love,
Beth

twenty

Finishing up last-minute details for my trip upstate, I sensed someone behind me and jumped. It was Linda.

"I didn't hear you come in."

"I tiptoed. Lisa's sleeping. Take this. You might need it to do or buy something special." She slipped some money into my open suitcase. Five ten-dollar bills.

"That's a lot of money."

"You worked hard this summer. You deserve it. And here's a letter for you."

It was from Jonathan. I hadn't remembered to look in the mailbox, I was so excited. Why would he send me a letter now? I was going to see him in less than twenty-four hours. Was he canceling? Wouldn't he have called?

"Don't looked so shocked. Don't you think I know that you're still involved with Jonathan?"

"I am?"

"Come on, Beth. I pick up the mail, too. You must think I'm really thick."

"Does Dad know?"

"No."

"How come? You know how he feels after all that went on?"

"He loves you, even though you think he doesn't. It's hard for him to see you growing up. Letting go. Especially when you've come into his life again."

"Are you going to tell him?"

"Are you going to see Jonathan?"

Should I lie? "I'm seeing him this weekend. Nance is visiting his friend Max. Her parents know."

"We'll keep it between us. Just leave me the address and a phone number this time."

"Okay." I sighed. "Why are you doing this?"

"I was your age once, with a boyfriend, too. Give us a call. For your father. He couldn't say goodbye. Early conference. But I know he wanted to."

Nance's parents' green station wagon pulled into the driveway, interrupting our conversation. Bicycles, water skis, and baggage were fastened to a rack on the top. I waved to Linda standing alone in the doorway. She looked pretty wearing a white cotton smocked dress, her light, sunny hair falling on her bare shoulders. Maybe I would have liked Linda if we hadn't been thrown together this way? I watched her through the car window, turning around a second time as we drove away. She waved, and remained, smiling.

When we stopped at a Hot Shoppe for gas and lunch, I raced into the bathroom, closed the door to the pay toilet, and sat down, ripping open Jonathan's letter.

Dear Beth,

Hope you receive this in time. Won't be able to see you Friday night, if you're up here by then. Max is calling Nance to make arrangements to hear us at Joe's Bar and Grill for Saturday night. Looking forward to seeing you then. Sorry about the rushed script.

Love, Jonathan

Why couldn't he make it? I felt set up again. Go slow, I thought. Go slow, Beth.

"Beth? It's Nance. We're ready to order."

"Be there in a minute."

I felt bad, but I didn't need to share all the soap-opera episodes of my life with Nance. I wasn't sure why, but that's the way it was. What I needed was time to think about what I was doing.

I didn't feel festive after reading Jonathan's letter. I spent Saturday with Nance on the lake, without even a phone call from him. After dinner, Nance borrowed my jasmine oil to dab behind her ears and on her neck. I applied some of her pale-brown sparkled eye shadow and stared in the mirror. My eyes were burning, holding back the tears. Nance danced around the room, her permed curls bobbing in the air. Her parents peeked in, said they were going for a walk, then playing in a bridge tournament, and we shouldn't come in too late. I was beginning to think that all parents should have that tattooed on their foreheads.

Max arrived in a beat-up yellow minibus that said CAMP WINAPASAKEE on the side door. We climbed in the front next to him. My sandals stuck to the floor from leftover bubblegum and Juicy Fruits. Nance leaned over to hug Max, letting out a groan as the stick shift dug into her thigh. He kissed her on the neck near her perfumed ear.

"How's life been treating you?" Max asked, looking at me.

"Okay," I answered.

"Okay?" he asked.

"Lay off," said Nance. "Beth has the jitters tonight."

"That's right. I forgot, I'm sorry. You and Jonathan had a falling-out."

"Drop it, Max."

I broke in. "It's okay, Nance. Max, is Jonathan seeing anyone else?"

Max evaded my question. "Do you have ID's?"

"No." We answered in unison.

"Maybe you won't need any. You both look eighteen."

Nance and I turned to each other, smiling confidently.

"We'll drink Shirley Temples." She grinned.

"No, thanks," I said.

"We're here. Joe's Bar and Grill. All the grease you can eat. With a salad bar, of course."

I stepped down and thought to myself: This is it.

Past the smoke, the dark blue and red lights, the overcrowded small round wooden tables and booths, I saw Jonathan leaning against a post, a hand resting on his back. I wanted to run up and rip that hand off him. But was Jonathan mine? To own?

Max grabbed our arms, pushing his way through throngs of people. Jonathan sipped some Rheingold out of a can. His blond, sun-streaked hair fell over the back of his collar. Love is a funny thing. You can wish for it, or wish it away, but it isn't something you can control. I still wanted Jonathan, in spite of the anger, hurt, and all. I tapped him on the back, quickly taking my hand away.

"Beth." He looked uncomfortable. Or was it me who was uptight?

"You're here, Beth," he repeated and bent down to kiss me. I didn't want it to feel the same, but it did. Good. Not good. Great. Jonathan really got to me. I was so nervous, I needed time to breathe.

"Where's the bathroom?" I asked, needing to be alone. Standing in front of the small, cracked sink, I threw cold water on my flushed cheeks. I looked for a paper towel, but the dispenser was empty. These places never even have toilet paper. Using some old tissues from my purse, I blotted my soggy forehead, and I brushed my hair while I took a long, hard look at myself. "It's going to be okay. Mom said I had inner strength." And I sighed.

Outside, the band was already playing. I edged into the booth alongside Nance and ordered a Tom Collins. Nance was guzzling a Singapore Sling. It turned out that the girl who had had her hand on Jonathan's back was the lead singer and a waitress in the hotel where Jonathan worked. She looked older, about twenty-one. Max told Nance while I had been in the bathroom that she lived up here year-round. Was I blowing this out of proportion? I wasn't sure of his feelings, or if anything was going on. What I did know was the way she looked and sang to him in this room full of people. I needed air. I was about to get up when these two yokels came over to me and Nance.

"You gals alone?" Before we had a chance to answer no, the gargantuan one with the d.a. yelled, "Hey, Shirl, get these two little honeys some beer. And a large pitcher for us. This is my friend Mac. I'm Pete." What else did I expect in a Joe's Bar but a Mac and a Pete?

"Big Mac?" I asked.

"I like that." He almost knocked me out of my seat. "A little lady with a sense of humor."

"If he calls me 'little' again . . ." I whispered to Nance. "I've gotta get out of here."

"And leave me alone with these apes!"

"Max is right over there."

"Max would be limp linguine in their hands."

"Then call a bouncer."

"What bouncer? They look like bouncers."

Nance lied to them that her father was the chief of police of Liberty, and would they please not tell anyone she was really underage? I laughed as I saw them quickly gathering their beer mugs. If only they knew he was really a salesman at House of Carpets. As I was leaving, I heard over the mike: "And our next number is dedicated to Beth."

Joe's Bar was right off the interstate highway. Out back, plastic garbage bags were stacked against the kitchen door, the exhaust fan blew stale smoke reeking of well-done hamburgers and oily fried potatoes. I walked along a dirt path, kicking pebbles, until I came to a small hill that sloped to a brook. Why couldn't everything turn out differently? I spread out my faded dungaree jacket and sat on a cold, flat rock, holding my knees to my chest. That special smell of the country surrounded me.

"Is this seat taken?" Jonathan asked, squatting down.

"How did you find me?"

"You left a trail of bread crumbs, Gretel."

"What song did you dedicate to me, then?"

"Just Like a Woman."

"Why?"

"Listen to the words. You didn't the first time."

> "Nobody feels any pain
> Tonight as I stand inside the rain . . ."

My bottom lip quivered as I turned away. The words melted together. I didn't want to hear, but they continued to come through.

"She takes just like a woman . . .
She makes love just like a woman . . .
And she aches just like a woman
But she breaks just like a little girl."

There was that word "little" again. The second
time tonight. Was I a girl-woman? Which one? Both?
And then I remembered the rest of the words as he
recited them.

"It was raining from the first
And I was dying there of thirst
So I came in here
And your long-time curse hurts
But what's worse
Is the pain in here
I can't stay in here
Ain't it clear that—
I just can't fit
Yes, I believe it's time for us to quit
When we meet again
Introduced as friends
Please don't let on that you knew me when—"

Jonathan rocked me in his arms.
"Did you sleep with her? The singer?"
"Why?"
"Never mind." The answer should have been
"no," not "why."
He put his arm around me. I tensed, but didn't
move away. Then he kissed my eyelids. My nose.
My lips. I couldn't kiss him back, but I held on tight-

er than I ever did. We made love on the cushioned moss. I lost myself in him. Distance had brought us closer together. There was a part of me that knew this was the last time, and another part that couldn't face it. Why was I doing this? Did it make any sense? I cringed at the idea of him being close like this with someone else.

"How did things get all screwed up? What were our letters all about? What happened, Jonathan? And when?"

"I slept with her once, just once."

"You could have screwed your head off, I don't care about how many times. You did it. Remember? Trust?"

He bowed his head and cried.

"Why were you mowing the lawn near my dad's that Saturday in April?"

"What?" He looked at me as though I was nuts.

"I just always wanted to know."

"For money. When I really needed the money, I skipped out on my music lessons, but not too often. Juilliard would drop my scholarship. That's what this is all about. The group. This summer. This gig. Money for my music. I told you. It comes first."

"I guess I never heard. It's coming through now."

Later, as I got into Max's minibus to leave, I touched the back of Jonathan's head, weaving his thick hair through my fingers.

Sunday night was a quiet drive back to the Island. I felt totally wiped out. Nance slept curled up on the seat next to me, snoring lightly.

Opening the door when I got back, I saw in the hall mirror my father putting his arms around Linda, kissing her neck. She was no longer Linda, my step-mother, someone I lived with; she was just a woman. A person who happened to love my father. Whom he loved back. I understood those feelings of wanting to be made love to and of loving someone. At the same time, nothing made any sense. There was something strange, missing. Mom. And I hurt the same as I did when my parents told me they weren't going to live together any more. I didn't want it to be true. And I ached the same as when I knew I'd never see my mother again. Why couldn't things stay the same? I wanted life back to the way it was. With Mom. With Jonathan. And it hurt to know things couldn't be that way again and there was nothing I could do about it. Ever.

twenty-one

The rest of the summer was pretty uneventful. The first week after I came back from the country, I had that aching feeling in my stomach each morning when I woke up. As the days went by, it disappeared.

I stayed home most nights after work, staring at my phone. Had Jonathan tried while I was out? When was I going to stop making excuses? For him? For Mom? Was he waiting for me to break down and call? I wanted to, but I didn't. Was it a game? Or were we growing apart? Too many hurts built up? Like Mom and Dad? It was all so confusing. Gradually, I started writing music again.

One good thing came out of the summer. Toward the end, Louise and Robin became my close friends. Bayview was feeling more like home. I looked forward to September, my senior year, sharing it with them. August 20 was Louise's birthday. Sweet sixteen. And never been kissed? What century was that from? Robin and I made her a special ice-cream cake in the shape of an airplane. We wrote "Fly Me" on it in pink icing. Robin had borrowed a car from her older brother, and the three of us went out to Jones Beach to celebrate. We played miniature golf and ate clam chowder. I thought of Mom and how she'd drive out just for that bowl of chowder. It wasn't so special, maybe it was even from a can, but it tasted better at the beach, warming my insides in the cold ocean breeze. And then I remembered Jonathan, his chicken-soup saga in my room. I missed them both.

I spent a weekend at Nance's. It was so strange seeing the old neighborhood, my old block, a new family in my house. At first, I thought I shouldn't go, but I couldn't erase Westchester from the map. There was a little girl sitting on my front stoop, playing jacks. A young woman came out of the door to check up, kissing her on the top of her head. Did this little girl sleep in my old room? Had they left my wallpaper up? Or repainted Mom's bright sun porch? I was afraid, even though I was tempted to ring the doorbell and ask, "Can I come in? I used to live here." The disappointment I might face, if things had changed, scared me. In the end, it was only four walls. The feelings about those objects my mother placed around the house, the memories of delicious smells, couldn't be taken away. They would always be there in my mind, and I could be a small child in those thoughts if I wanted to. I just didn't want to go back any more. The little girl looked up, smiled, and waved. Behind her was a shiny new mailbox. I turned around, waved back to the little girl, who was being sheltered in by her mother, and realized strange clothes would be hanging in Mom's closet.

Nance set me up on a blind date. We doubled. He was like processed American cheese. His idea of a fun evening was going to Bowlarama, Burger King for a whopper, which I didn't eat, and watching *The Midnight Special* on TV with a sausage hero in his lap. He made me feel worse. This date wasn't where I was at. My first time with Jonathan had been so wonderful. Would I ever have those feelings again? I looked forward to going home to Bayview, even though I had fun kidding about the date with Nance.

Jonathan called when he got back from the Catskills, but I no longer felt the same. I hadn't been waiting for his call. He told me he was thinking of buying an old black Volvo, like in the gangster movies. What happened to the money he was saving for college? For his music? Well, it wasn't something I had to think about any more.

Near Labor Day, Carolyn and Arthur Neely, old friends of my parents', came to visit us. We hadn't seen them in a long time. It was strange seeing Carolyn talking and joking with Linda in the kitchen as she scraped off the uneaten potato peels and steak bones into the garbage pail. Carolyn arranged little cakes she'd brought on some of my mother's old dishes, wedding presents my parents had received. Why had Dad taken them? Someday I'll ask for them when I set up my own home. Linda asked if Carolyn wanted tea or coffee. Mom would have known she could drink only milk. Would they become good friends? Would Linda know Carolyn's habits and secrets, too?

When dessert was on the table, Dad said, "This should be a celebration."

"What's the occasion?" Arthur asked.

"My wife's going back to work this fall in a publishing house."

"Congratulations! How wonderful to be able to raise a child and work. How are you going to do it?" asked Carolyn.

I loved getting this news bulletin filtered down through Carolyn's and Arthur's questions. Why were they celebrating with them?

"When did you find out about the job?" I asked, facing Linda.

"Recently."

"Why didn't you tell me?"

"I was going to."

"I was home all day yesterday."

"I didn't think it would affect you this way."

"Well, it does." I raised my voice. "How *are* you going to work it out?"

"Three days in the office. Two here."

"It sounds too good to be true. The best of both worlds," sighed Carolyn.

"Oh, a part-time job," exclaimed Arthur.

"No. A full-time one. My space is divided. I'm not."

"What about Lisa?" I asked.

"A woman in town will watch her those three days."

"Day care?" Carolyn said it as though it was a dirty word.

"Call it what you want. I call it a loving person who helps me with my child while I'm away. And Lisa gets to be with other young children. I think it will be fine after we all deal with the separation."

"Doesn't sound so awful." Dad grinned. "They only torture them on Tuesdays. I'm behind Linda. If she's happy, I am. And then Lisa will be, too. Right?"

"Right," said Linda definitively.

"Who will make dinner each night?" I asked.

"Will you excuse us a minute?" Linda beckoned me out to the kitchen. Dad followed. That was out of character for them.

"What's troubling you?" asked Linda.

"I want to know how much is going to be on me?"

"Listen, Beth, calm down. Linda and I have discussed it. You're not going to become Cinderella, if that's what all these questions are about. I'll lay it out for you simply. Someone is going to come clean every other week, and we'll all pitch in to help, too. Lisa is taken care of. The mother's helper can baby-sit sometimes. Maybe you can, too. I'll try and catch an early train, instead of one at eight or nine, on the days that Linda's working."

"You've got it all planned."

"We have to," said Linda. "What do you want?"

"If it sounds too pat, I can't help it. You asked what we've got worked out. This is it. We'll see how it goes. As a family. I'm trying, Beth. I can't do any more than that," said my father.

I hated to admit it to myself, I certainly wouldn't to them, but they were right.

"Oops! We left the Neelys out there," said Linda. She lifted my hair off my shoulders, and looked at me. "Don't worry. You take everything so hard. It will work out."

I hugged Carolyn goodbye and went out for a bicycle ride in one of the last nights of summer. I rode down to the beach where Jonathan and I always went, watched the gulls, and thought. The big shocker of this summer was Linda. She had changed the most. Mellowed out. Or was it me? She had given me the chance to see this thing through with Jonathan, without standing in my way. Maybe we had finally reached a truce?

twenty-two

Yellow autumn leaves dusted the sidewalk. Jonathan bumped into me, looking his gorgeous self in a down vest.

"How have you been?"

"Fine," I answered.

"I haven't seen you in school."

"I've been here. Guess we're in different classes."

"How's the music?"

"Okay. And yours?"

"Okay. I've thought about you often. Could we be friends?"

"I don't think I'm the type to be friends, afterwards. Do you know what I mean?" I asked.

"I don't know if I am, either. Thought I'd give it a try."

We went in opposite directions. I turned around to look at him. He didn't wave back over his shoulder this time.

When I returned after school from practicing the piano, Linda was in Dad's den, which was now her office besides a sewing room.

"I'm home," I said, poking my head in. Home. Would the word ever sound right?

"Could you put up the chicken? At 350 degrees. There's carrot cake in the refrigerator."

I was walking up to my room, holding a glass of milk and the cake, when Linda put down her papers and looked up. "Come on in. Let's talk."

"What about?" I asked, hedging in the doorway.

"Oh. Chew the fat."

Hesitantly, I balanced the plate on my knees as I rested my sneakers on the ottoman near Dad's recliner. The last time I had spent more than five minutes in this room was when Dad and I had had the big argument over Mom. The phone rang. Relieved, I ran upstairs to get it, but it was the wrong number. When I put the receiver down, Linda was sitting in my rocker.

"You've done such nice things with this room. Nicer than when it was just a sewing room. I love the wallpaper and this chair." She rocked back and forth. "There are times I'm sorry, Beth, I haven't been there for you as much as you think I should have. I've been busy with Lisa."

It was the first time I had heard her say she was sorry.

"Sometimes I wish I felt closer to you, but I can't. It's awful to admit, but I can't make those feelings happen. I don't know how to say this without sounding awkward, but I'll try to be honest. Maybe it isn't fair, but I didn't carry you around in my stomach for nine months. You didn't cause me morning sickness. You didn't exhaust me. Or kick me. I didn't feel your foot inside my rib cage. I dreamed of the time when I could turn over, put my head on the pillow, and sprawl out on the sheets. I didn't give up sleeping on my stomach for you. I did for Lisa. Do you understand?"

"It sounds like you hate her."

"Hate her?" repeated Linda. "The bond I feel is incredible. I didn't even know those feelings existed in me. I could kill to protect her. I don't know if I would do that for you, or even myself. I feel I've given a lot this past year. I expected one child, I got two. I know it hurts, and it's lousy, but what I said is what I feel."

Linda moved toward me on the shag rug as if to hug me, but I tensed. "I'm not ready." As I turned a shredded tissue around my finger, the tears wouldn't stop. Where were they all coming from? Linda tried to touch me again. I didn't have the energy to resist. Tears rolled down her cheeks, too. Was Linda crying for me?

"Let it out," she whispered.

"I got your blouse soaked."

"It's just a blouse."

"But it's silk, and you're such a fussbudget."

Neither of us said a word. I tried to talk, but I still felt choked up. It was quiet in the room.

"You know . . ." I started and trailed off, sniffing as my chest heaved in and out. I tried again. "You know, I haven't cried the whole time. Since my mother died. I didn't cry for her then. Am I crying for her now? Could that be?"

"I think so, Beth."

I sighed. It was a deep breath. I sighed again and again. Then stopped. Was I done? Was the mourning period that had never begun over? Not really over, would it ever be completely over? The pain, the hurt, the sadness, the anger that had consumed me finished? Could I ever feel for Linda? With my hand I grasped hers. She smiled. "I think I do love you, Beth. Not like my own child, in a different way. Somewhere between a daughter and a friend."

"I'm not sure if I can love you." This time it wasn't to hurt her. "I hope it'll change. Sometimes I need a mother. Aunt Ellen is good for that, but I don't live with her. I live here. With you and Dad."

"I understand. I'm not making excuses, but I was a single woman. Thirty-four with no commitments. Now I have a family. I can't do a simple thing like take a bath or shower when I feel like it, or even go to the bathroom alone without little fingers pawing me. The only time I had to myself was when I was asleep, which was interrupted when Lisa was first born for feedings, and now for listening for Lisa in my dreams. I wish just once you had offered to take care of her. To give me something. So I could walk out of this house being Linda, and not always Lisa's mother."

"I couldn't, I just couldn't. How could I give to you?"

She said nothing.

"No one gave to me."

"Oh God, Beth. I've given so much."

"Given up," I said, "not given."

"Maybe I was expecting too much?"

"I have needs, too."

"I know," she said softly. "You've grown this last year, learned to come through for yourself the hard way."

"What can be worse than finding your own mother dead?"

Linda cast down her eyes. Suddenly I wasn't so sure I was ready to be grown-up and take responsibility for myself, which meant also feeling bad about how I had acted. Had anyone walked in the front door, up the staircase to my room, they might have thought they had interrupted two friends in the middle of an intimate conversation. I glanced up at the skylight. This room had become more my own. Behind the leaves of the trees the sky was a cold white. Nothing moved.

"Maybe it will rain tomorrow," I said.

"Maybe," said Linda, wiping away a tear.

She went downstairs to begin dinner, and I followed to help her.

Later that night, when I got into bed, one of the things I thought about that made me the saddest was that my mother never gave me a last chance to tell her that I loved her. When you know someone is dying, you can say goodbye, and all the things you ever wanted to say, or just give them a look that says how you feel. Our eyes never met in that moment's glance when we both knew and understood how the other felt. I whispered to the four walls in my bedroom, "Mom, wherever you are, I love you."

twenty-three

When I woke up the next morning, it was raining. Another Saturday. I could stay under the covers. It was the first morning in a long time that I didn't feel a sense of loss. It was six-thirty, and just beginning to get light outside.

I slipped my yellow slicker on over my jeans and a ratty T-shirt, the one I had slept in, and walked out into the rain. It was a light rain, a drizzle that tickled my nose, cold. Every time the wind swayed the large maple trees, I felt a chill and hugged my body. The air smelled of wild scallions, ferns, and moldy, wet leaves. Rain washed the dirt off the rocks and stones, smoothing them over, polishing them like Linda's waxed terra-cotta floor. A salamander slithered through the leaves. If only I was four again, walking with Mom in a state park, trying to catch salamanders. But that part of my life was over.

. My feet sank slightly into the ground with each step as I walked home for breakfast. The world felt open. The legacy that Mom left me, to hide from life, not take chances or follow dreams, was not my own—living felt too good. I liked to walk in the rain, or stay inside and write music. To do what pleased me was what I needed. Rain meant peace for me, not grayness or depression, as it did for Mom.

Alone no longer felt bad. It didn't mean loneliness; it meant I belonged to myself. It was hard to have the kind of assurance Jonathan had, but I was going to try. I no longer felt like a victim. Things had changed, but, like watching an hour hand, I couldn't see them move.

As I reached the house, I could see through the window Lisa in her antique hand-caned oak high chair. Dad and Linda were seated at the table. The scene was right out of an ad: cereal box, milk container, orange-juice pitcher, fruit, checked tablecloth. I swung through the back door and hung up my coat.

"We haven't started yet," said Dad.

Water dripped on the floor. Linda stared at the puddles. "I'll clean it up," I said.

"The floor has to be done tomorrow, anyway."

I bent down to blot the water up with paper towels. Dad pulled the chair away from the table.

"Breakfast is getting cold."

"I'm starving," I said, wondering how cold cereal could get cold. Then I saw the bluish-purple liquid pasted on Lisa's face. Blueberry pancakes. I started to laugh at her. Lisa flung some cereal in my hair as I sat down to eat. It was the first time she'd done that that I didn't want to take the bowl and push it down on her golden curls, as Mr. Lyn Belvedere, a male nanny, did in an old movie, called *Sitting Pretty*, I had watched on TV with Mom.

"You little devil, you!" I shouted.

Lisa gurgled. Her two front teeth were like little pearls popping up from her gums. Why hadn't I noticed them before? They were adorable. She started playing peekaboo and then wrapped her tiny hand around one of my fingers, holding on to it tightly, with her pink pudgy knuckles bulging.

"Do you want to come shopping with us today?" asked Dad. "We're going to the mall to get Lisa a walker."

"I'm practicing the piano at school later. Thanks anyway," I said.

"On a Saturday? You must be serious. Do you practice a lot?" he asked.

"Don't you remember, Ma had Grandma's old piano, the upright? I played it all the time."

"Why didn't we ship it here? Instead of putting it in storage? Why didn't you say something?"

"I didn't think of it at the time." Why hadn't I? Was it because, if I brought the piano, it would have been admitting that this was home and I was staying here? But I had cheated myself.

"Beth, if it's important to you, we can take it out of storage."

"Where would we put it?" I asked.

"We'll find a place."

"Maybe I should have the piano here. I've been told I'm pretty talented by my music teacher, Mr. Wheldon. I started writing music again this past term." I thought of Jonathan. Had he gotten into Juilliard on early admission?

"How ambitious," said Linda.

"We'd like to hear you play," said Dad.

He was trying hard. They both were. I was surprised at his interest. He was so wrapped up with his family and work. Maybe I hadn't given him a chance?

"We would," added Linda.

"Well, I'm working on some stuff for a recital at Bleeker next month. Would you both like to come?" I was almost sorry I'd said anything. Maybe it was too soon to share my music with them. I looked up as I heard drops marching on the roof, falling down the gutter.

"It is raining today," said Linda.

"I hope I don't have to plant those bulbs again," said Dad.

I watched him slice strawberries into his dry cereal and realized I wasn't going to change him. My father was always going to be the kind of person I couldn't hug or kiss or talk to easily. But in a peculiar sort of way, my father was alive and there, could be counted on in a crisis, and my mother killed herself and wasn't there at all.

I rose from the table. "I'll be leaving soon."

"Work hard," said my father.

"See you later," said Linda.

They both turned to Lisa.

I walked out the front door. Sticking my tongue out to taste the rain, I swung around in a circle and stomped in a puddle like a little kid. And laughed. "Beth Corey, life ain't so bad." I ran for the bus, holding on to my music.

About the Author

Jane Breskin Zalben is the author and illustra-
tor of many books for younger readers, includ-
ing *Will You Count the Stars With Me?* and
Oh Simple! This is her first novel. Her second
novel, *Here's Looking at You, Kid,* has been
recently published. Jane Breskin Zalben lives
on Long Island with her husband and two
children.